"I guess I'll see you in the morning," Sierra told him, reaching for the doorknob.

But Dante made no move to leave. Against her better judgment, Sierra lifted her face to look at his, immediately realizing what a mistake that was. The way Dante was looking at her had her knees weakening.

Dante's eyes, hooded and dark with emotion, landed on her lips. Without knowing she intended it, she stepped closer to where he stood, their mouths now barely an inch apart. That tempting scent of his aftershave teased her, had her mouth going dry.

"Sierra." Her name on his lips sent a shudder through her core.

"Yes?"

He blinked, swallowed. Then he leaned toward her. The next instant somehow his lips were on hers. Time stopped. As did her heart beating in her chest.

He tasted like citrus and mint and some exotic spice she wouldn't be able to name.

He tasted as good as she'd always known he would.

Dear Reader,

One of the hardest things I can imagine is to feel as if you don't belong in the world of the person you love. To look upon that person and know that another might fit better in the life they inhabit. In *The Prince's Safari Temptation*, Sierra Compari has to endure this very anguish throughout most of her life. She's known Prince Dante since they were both children, started falling in love with him during her teen years. But Dante will soon be crowned king, and Sierra cannot see herself in the role of queen. She's too independent, too focused on her career and simply not polished enough.

Dante married the woman everyone assumed was perfect for him, a woman born to be a royal. But his soul yearned for another, longed for a way in which he could have followed his heart and chosen the woman he's always loved instead—Sierra.

When fate gives them a chance to choose differently, will they be able to overcome all that stands in their way and pick the path that brings them together?

I hope you enjoy reading Dante and Sierra's story to find out the answer.

Nina Singh

The Prince's Safari Temptation

Nina Singh

H HARLEQUIN

Romance

HARLEQUIN®

Romance™

Recycling programs
for this product may
not exist in your area.

ISBN-13: 978-1-335-59639-0

The Prince's Safari Temptation

Harlequin Enterprises ULC
22 Adelaide St. West, 41st Floor
Toronto, Ontario M5H 4E3, Canada
www.Harlequin.com

Printed in U.S.A.

Nina Singh lives just outside Boston, Massachusetts, with her husband, children and a very rambunctious Yorkie. After several years in the corporate world, she finally followed the advice of family and friends to "give the writing a go, already." She's oh-so-happy she did. When not at her keyboard, she likes to spend time on the tennis court or golf course. Or immersed in a good read.

For my mother, who brilliantly adapted to a world in which she at first did not belong.

Praise for
Nina Singh

"A captivating holiday adventure!
Their Festive Island Escape by Nina Singh
is a twist on an enemies-to-lovers trope and is
sure to delight. I recommend this book to anyone....
It's fun, it's touching and it's satisfying."

—*Goodreads*

CHAPTER ONE

PRINCE DANTE ANGILERA made his way down the cavernous hallway in the north wing of the main castle, his shadow casting a long dark path behind him. He'd been summoned. Maman had messaged him before dawn this morning to meet her bright and early as she took her breakfast on the north garden patio facing the majestic mountains of Nocera, the island kingdom Dante was heir to. Located in the Mediterranean, several miles from Cyprus, Nocera marketed itself as a prime vacation spot throughout the year, but particularly during the summer season.

He knew the reason she needed to speak to him. And the tightness of anxiety gripped his chest as it came to mind. His father, the king, had been experiencing heart palpitations for the past week. The doctors were concerned but not alarmed. Yet.

Arriving at the patio, Dante found Maman sipping tea from a steaming delicate porcelain cup. No doubt it was at least her third or fourth given the hour. She was scrolling hastily through her tablet and taking notes in a leather-bound notebook with her gold-casted pen. A devoted supporter of many causes, Maman always had one project or another on her plate.

Hence the reason for this visit. The king's heart issues had thrown a major glitch in one of her most important endeavors. The prince and she needed to figure out what to do about it.

A wide, friendly smile spread across her face when she looked up to find him approaching. She gestured with her cup to the chair next to her and motioned for Vito, their trusted butler, to bring Dante's cup of espresso.

"How is Papa this morning?" Dante asked, unnecessarily as he'd been adamant that the rotating group of royal doctors keep him updated at all times on his father's condition.

Her lips tightened and she frowned. "The same. But now, on top of his health concerns, he's started to become restless and bored."

Dante shrugged. "Well, he will have to deal with his boredom. He is not to strain himself in any way until the physicians get his condition under control."

"You and I know that. Which brings me to why I called you down here."

Dante didn't have to guess.

"The dignitary tour for your and Papa's conservation foundation. I suppose it will have to be canceled now."

She blinked at him. "But I don't want to cancel it, my dear son."

Dante didn't bother to ask if she intended to go alone. If he knew his *maman*, there was no way she would leave his father's side at a time like this, when his health was in question. Dante's parents were the rare exception when it came to arranged marriages. They genuinely cared for and loved each other. Somehow, they'd found the wherewithal to combine duty and love. So different from his own lot in life. His marriage had been a failure from the start. A failure that had ended in tragedy.

"Then what…?" he began, but didn't finish the sentence as realization dawned. Of course, how could he not have seen this coming? "You'd like me to go on the safari in your stead."

She nodded slowly. "It's the only way that makes sense. We already had to postpone this trip once."

His mother was referring to the accident, the tragedy, two years ago that had claimed the life of his wife, the princess who would have been the future queen.

The kingdom's papers still found his marriage, as well as the accident, an endless source of content. At some point, they'd deemed him the ever grieving widower prince, speculating whether there would be a princess again at some future point. Dante hadn't so much as had a date since Rula's passing. He felt a twinge of guilt. The people of the kingdom and the worldwide tabloids attributed his lack of a romantic life on speculation that he was still heartbroken over the loss of his spouse. Everyone assumed Dante had married for love as well as duty.

If they only knew.

The truth was a bit less fairy tale worthy, the reality being that Dante had failed as a husband. His wife had been unhappy. Maybe she'd guessed that his heart wasn't in the union, and she'd paid for the mistake of their failed marriage with her life.

An image of a smiling face with bright hazel eyes and golden tanned skin formed in his mind's eye. Dante mentally pushed the image and the wayward thoughts away. No use dwelling on any of it now. Never mind that the guilt of his failings would haunt him the rest of his life.

The trip was certainly going to put a major dent in his schedule. He had meetings lined up all next week with various ministers and his most trusted economists about the kingdom's current political and financial status. He supposed that some of that could be done remotely, even from a far corner of Africa, but it wasn't going to be easy. Dante sighed with resignation. If he knew his *maman*, there was no point in arguing.

"All right. I'll go start making the arrangements. Please have Vito bring my espresso to my office."

Before he could rise from his chair, Dante noted the expression on Maman's face. His mother's eyes scanned his face expectedly. Clearly, there was more she wanted to say. "Why do I get the feeling there's something else?" Something he distinctly got the impression he wasn't going to like.

"Your father and I have discussed it, and we've decided that a true representation of Nocera will have to include more than just the crown prince on such a trip."

Dante didn't like the direction this conversation was headed. Her words could only mean one thing. "I won't be going alone?"

She shook her head. "Think about it, dear. Many of these visits involve ceremonies, meetings and formal events. Both men and women will be present. You will need a prominent female presence to complete the delegation, just as your father and I would have been."

Only one person made sense as a possibility. Perna, their trusted royal aide and decades-long employee of the royal family. "Has anyone told Perna that she'll be traveling to Africa in a few short weeks?"

To his surprise, Maman shook her head once again. "No, not Perna. Someone a bit more representative as an extended member of the royal family. Besides, Perna is needed here. You know how much your father depends on our most trusted aide."

"Then who?"

Maman lifted an elegant shoulder. "Someone who's worked at the palace in the past, someone who will represent the Angilera name with dignity. Someone who knows us well and has her entire life."

Alarm bells began to ring in Dante's head as his mother's words echoed through his mind...

An extended member of the royal family... Someone who's worked at the palace in the past...

Maman meant her goddaughter, a woman he'd known since childhood.

No, that had to be wrong. She couldn't possibly mean to suggest—

But she did. The name his mother uttered was the last one he wanted to hear as a possibility. The same vision of the smiling face once again intruded behind his eyes.

This time, there was no pushing it away.

* * *

"You've outdone yourself with this one." The voice came from above her head as Sierra adjusted the hem of the cocktail dress she'd just completed that morning, mere moments before the model had arrived for the fitting.

Camille, the model in question, was one of Sierra's favorite to work with. The two women had grown somewhat close during the period of time Sierra had been hired as a sketch artist for the House of Perth and her recent promotion to assistant designer.

"Thanks," she responded, rising to stand then stretching her aching back. She'd been huddled over her desk then the sewing machine for most of the night. Now, her muscles were screaming in protest.

"One down," she added. With several more to go. Darned if she knew how or when the rest would come to her. She'd been creatively blocked for longer than she wanted to admit, with no designs coming to mind that she would deem worthy of putting down on paper, let alone cutting fabric for.

On top of the creative block, there was also a distraction to deal with. How to respond to her godmother, Her Majesty Naila Angilera, Queen of Nocera.

Sierra stifled a giggle. Calling the honorable

queen of an island kingdom a mere distraction seemed beyond silly of her. If she were smart, she would drop everything she was doing and respond to the queen right away. But Sierra couldn't seem to bring herself to do so. The queen wanted a personal face-to-face visit. For what, Sierra couldn't begin to guess. But she had a season to prepare for with no ideas to show for it. She had to show the mega designer house in New York's fashion district she was lucky enough to work for that she had the chops to deliver.

Besides, Nocera seemed worlds away, a different lifetime. Aside from sporadic calls from her busy parents, she hardly thought about her old life in the tiny island kingdom.

Right, a nagging voice teased. As if her hesitation about traveling to her old home nation didn't have everything to do with the risk of seeing *him* again. "Him" being Crown Prince Dante Angilera, her once best friend's widowed husband.

"What's the matter?" Camille asked, drawing her back to the here and now. "You've got a faraway look in your eyes and your forehead is drawn tight."

Sierra made a concentrated effort to smooth out her facial features.

Camille gave her a critical look. "That's not

much better. You're going to get several wrinkles if you insist on scrunching your face that way."

Sierra sighed and rubbed at her hairline, as if she could smooth away the dreaded wrinkles the other woman warned about.

"I just have a lot on my mind."

"Please tell me it involves a tall, dark and handsome someone you have yet to tell me about."

Sierra chuckled. "Not quite."

Though perhaps Camille's statement was more accurate than she wanted to admit. But the truth was, despite her colleagues and a few of the models' repeated attempts to set her up on dates, Sierra didn't have much of a dating life. Or one at all, for that matter.

There was too much to do; her job was too demanding, taking all of her energy and time to come up with new ideas and designs. She refused to speculate as to any other possible reason.

"You know," Camille began, "my cousin's friend from the Upper East Side just broke up with his girlfriend—"

Sierra cut her off before she could say any more. Another blind date was the last thing she wanted to attempt right now. "Thanks, but no."

Camille hopped off the block and began

carefully removing the dress, starting with the delicate straps. In moments, she was down to wearing nothing but a delicate lace thong, despite the myriad of staff and others roaming about the room. No one so much as stared.

The modeling life didn't lend to shyness or modesty. These women had to get dressed and undressed in mere seconds during runway shows. The lot of them were professionals who'd been modeling since their teen years.

"Well, if you change your mind, yada yada."

"Sure," Sierra answered with smile, not meaning it in the least. The chances she was going to let Camille or anyone else for that matter set her up were slim to none.

Camille threw on the tiny tank top and fitted jean leggings she'd walked in with earlier that afternoon, then strode away after throwing an air kiss in Sierra's general direction.

She simply wasn't interested in pursuing anything romantic. What was the point anyway? Her dear friend had fallen in love and married a literal prince. What had it gotten her in the end?

Her eyes began to sting with the memory of her loss, and Sierra had to suppress a sniffle. Guilt combined with loss was a potent combination. But she had nothing to feel guilty for, damn it. One couldn't be faulted for thoughts and emotions they'd never acted on.

So why did her heart feel so heavy?

Sierra drew in a deep breath and tried to wrangle her emotions. She couldn't be seen crying here, for heaven's sake. It wasn't very professional.

Someone cleared their throat behind her. Not quite ready to turn around and reveal the potential evidence of tears in her eyes, she sucked in a breath and summoned her voice.

"You're back. Did you want to try on the dress again? I was just about to hang it on the completed rack."

She didn't receive an answer for several beats. Then, "I don't think it's quite my color. A bit too much of a pastel." A deep, masculine voice had spoken behind her. Definitely not Camille.

Sierra's blood froze in her veins and her breath locked in her chest. It couldn't be; she had to be imagining things.

But then the scent of mint and sandalwood reached her nostrils, and Sierra knew her mind wasn't playing tricks on her. This was all too real.

She would know that voice and that scent anywhere, heaven help her.

"Hey, Sisi."

Any remnants of doubt fled her mind at the two simple words. Only one person had ever called her that.

* * *

Dante almost felt guilty for the way Sierra's eyes grew wide with shock when she finally turned around and saw him standing three feet away.

"Dante. What are you doing here?"

He began to answer, but she waved it away with her hand. Apparently, it was rhetorical.

"Never mind. I guess that's what I get for not responding to the queen right away." She answered her own question. "She sends her son in person."

Dante tried to remain unaffected at seeing Sierra Compari again. She appeared the same, yet so very different. Her face had matured yet remained as beautiful as he remembered. She wore her hair straight now, the silky auburn strands flowing past her shoulders. Her catlike hazel eyes remained as bright as he remembered. And right now, they were boring right through him.

"On the contrary," he told her. "No one sent me. I'm here of my own will. Completely."

She crossed her arms in front of her chest. "You could have given me a heads-up."

Dante took a step toward her. The scent of her familiar rose and vanilla perfume tickled his nose. "Would you have agreed to see me if I'd announced my visit beforehand?"

Her answer was simple and direct. "No."

"I thought so."

"I was going to reply to Her Grace's emails soon enough. You hardly needed to fly halfway across the world."

Dante shrugged. "Maybe so. I thought it would be considerate of me to do so. The least I could do was to sit down with you in person. Given that we're the ones requesting a favor of you."

She visibly swallowed. "Favor? What kind of favor?"

Dante glanced about the room. Various women were in the stages of undress. Racks of clothing were being rolled from one end of the room to the other. A high-tempo techno song played loudly in the background, heavy bass thudding through the room.

"Perhaps we could go somewhere a bit more private to discuss it."

Her chin lifted defiantly. "Whatever you have to say, you can say it right here."

Dante should have expected a refusal. Sierra was…well, she was Sierra. Try as he might, he couldn't help but compare her to his former wife. Whereas Rula had always been gentle and soft-spoken, Sierra was always straight and to the point. She didn't mince words when she wanted to get her point across. And she was often stubborn. So very stubborn.

He made a show of glancing at his watch.

"It's just past noon. Surely you can get away for lunch."

"What makes you think I haven't eaten already?"

"Have you?"

She didn't deign to give him a response. "I have a lot to do, Dante."

He could be stubborn as well. Especially given the stakes. "This won't take long, Sisi. Believe me, we need to have this discussion. The sooner the better."

Her lips tightened. "Fine."

His shoulders sagged with relief. The sooner he got this over with, the sooner he could begin to try to convince her to go along with his mother's idea.

"Great. I have a suite rented at the Grand Ritz. We can eat there. There's a car waiting outside."

"Fine," she repeated, turning on her heel. "But just know that I'm only agreeing to hear you out because it's really the queen who's asking." She threw the words over her shoulder.

He had absolutely no doubt. The queen always had a lot of sway with Sierra Compari. Dante could only hope that hadn't changed.

Within minutes, they'd arrived at the hotel and were riding the private elevator to the suite of rooms on the top floor.

Dante couldn't recall the last time he and Sierra had been alone together, let alone in such tight quarters. That familiar scent of hers was wreaking havoc on his senses.

He'd taken great comfort in that scent once. Before circumstances and fate had cost him the friendship of the only woman who had ever truly known him for who he was, and not the crown prince of Nocera.

He led her out of the elevator when they reached the top floor and past the foyer into the dining area. A table had already been set up with polished, glinting silverware and bone china plates. A server appeared immediately, wheeling a cart of platters full of steaming food.

Dante pulled a chair out for Sierra and sat down next to her as the man served their meal.

"What's this all about?" Sierra demanded to know as soon as the other man had left. She hadn't so much as glanced at the stuffed lobster shell placed on the plate before her.

So much for actually eating lunch.

Dante took a deep breath before beginning. "The king and queen have been scheduled for quite some time to visit a few different locations as part of a tour to call attention to my mother's foundation."

Sierra nodded then took a bit of her French

roll, chewing slowly. "Environmental and wild-life conservation."

He nodded. "That's right. The tour was to highlight all the ways people can be environmentally conscious despite where they live throughout the world. Even in places such as the African savanna. And that animals are an integral part of the environment they're native to."

"I know all this, Dante," she said, her voice holding no small amount of impatience.

Better to just spit it out, Dante figured. "It turns out they won't be able to go, after all." He wasn't ready to tell her exactly why just yet. Guilting Sierra into making this decision because of concern for his father didn't sit right with him.

Concern washed over his features so he went on before she could ask. "I'll be going in their stead."

"I see." She took another bite of her baguette roll. "What does any of this have to do with me, then?"

"The queen would much prefer if I didn't go alone. She thinks I need someone to accompany me. Preferably female. Someone who can represent Nocera as a true daughter of the kingdom."

Once again, Sierra's eyes grew wide at his words. She looked as if she couldn't decide whether to swallow the morsel of bread in her mouth or spit it out instead. Luckily, she decided on the former.

"You can't possibly be suggesting what I think you are."

There was no other way than to just say what he'd come all the way to New York to say. "The queen thinks you should be that person, Sisi. We are asking you to accompany me."

Sierra's mouth went dry and she dropped her half-eaten roll on the table. She'd suddenly lost all her appetite, which was quite a shame. It really had been quite a delicious baguette, crusty on the outside and flaky soft on the inside. Not to mention how gourmet the seafood entrée looked. But she had more important things to contend with right now than an empty stomach.

She couldn't have heard Dante correctly. "I'm sorry, I could have sworn you just said that you wanted me to accompany you on some kind of dignitary trip on behalf of the royal couple."

His response to that was nothing whatsoever. He just thinned his lips and continued to stare at her. It took all of Sierra's will to remain calm and unaffected. Of all the gall.

Slowly with one smooth motion, she pushed her chair back from the table and rose to her feet. "It appears you've wasted your time, Prince Dante. As well as a pointless trip halfway across the world. Maybe you can see some sights to make up for it. The Statue of Liberty, perhaps."

Dante sighed deeply before speaking. "I take it your initial reaction is to say no."

"Initial and final, I'm afraid. Now, if you'll excuse me." But she hadn't made it more than a couple feet away from the table before he'd reached her side. Long, tan fingers gripped her elbow gently.

"Just hear me out, Sierra. That's all I ask."

"Why?"

He tilted his head, took a step closer. That familiar cologne of his taking her mind to a past she had no business thinking of. So much had happened since then that she couldn't allow herself to forget.

Dante answered as if he'd just read her mind. "For old times' sake?"

Sierra felt herself bristle from head to toe. "What's that supposed to mean?"

"Would traveling with me be so bad?"

"You do not want me to answer that question." Neither did she. Because she didn't even want to think about it—flying halfway across the world with him, seeing him every day. The whole problem was that it probably wouldn't be bad at all. Not in the least. And she so couldn't go there.

He let go of her, pinched the bridge of his

nose. "We were friends once, Sierra. The best of friends."

She chuckled. "Right. That's why I'm hearing from you now after all these months. When you need me to do something for you." Rula's funeral service was the last time they'd so much as spoken. And that had hardly been any kind of true conversation given the cloud of grief hanging over them both.

His eyebrows lifted. "Did you want to hear from me?"

Damn it. The answer to that question was beside the point. The point was he hadn't made any kind of attempt.

He blew out a long breath. "Don't leave. At least finish your lunch."

"No, thank you. I seem to have lost my appetite."

"Look, this was the queen's idea. Did you expect me to flat-out refuse to try to honor her wish?"

"I expected you to try to have her see reason."

He lifted an eyebrow. "Her reasoning is quite sound. You are a daughter of Nocera. You've done work for the queen before you left the kingdom and relocated. Some of that work involved the very foundation we'll be supporting with this trip."

Sierra hated that he was making sense. NEWEF,

the Nocera Environmental and Wildlife Ecological Foundation, was one of the royal family's most esteemed organizations worldwide. "Nevertheless, you should have tried to persuade her this was a bad idea, Dante."

He laughed briefly. "You really have been gone too long if you think that would have worked on Maman."

Sierra pointed a finger at him, nearly jabbing his chest. "It's too bad my dear friend isn't around anymore to join you on such travels."

His obvious and sharp flinch sent a rush of guilt through her. That was a low blow. Dante's stricken expression had her wishing she could somehow take the words back. They were harsh words, admittedly unfair. Dante might not have been what Rula had needed in a husband—he always seemed distant with her the few times Sierra had seen them together—but no one person could be faulted for the car crash that had claimed Rula's life. Rula had been the one driving late at night in a foreign country without any support staff or bodyguards. No one could guess why she'd gone off on her own. Sierra had figured she had needed to get away, needed some time to herself away from the demands placed on her as the future queen. But the truth was anyone's guess. In any case, it was needlessly reckless of her friend, and the impulsive trip had cost Rula her life.

Dante stepped away from her, his eyes shuttered now in shadow. "Just think about it, Sisi. That's all I ask. I'll be here until tomorrow afternoon." He motioned to the elevator. "Stewart will see you out."

The same car was waiting for her when she made it down to the street. The driver stood next to the vehicle with the passenger door open.

She shook her head in his direction. "No, thanks. I think I'll just walk and get some air."

The driver merely shut the door in response, gave her a friendly tip-of-the-hat wave.

Sierra rushed down the sidewalk, thinking of no particular destination. Her mind was a jumbled mess of thoughts, her heart a jumbled mess of emotions.

The nerve of that man. To shock her by simply showing up at the studio and then to throw such a request at her. What was he thinking? He had to know in advance that her answer would be a resounding and flat "no."

So why had he come here unannounced? Dante wasn't spontaneous or impulsive by any means. There had to be a piece of the puzzle she was missing, something he hadn't told her.

She was still pondering that question when she found herself entering Central Park. Being here always helped to clear her head. Something about the open air and all the strangers going about their business served as a balm for frazzled nerves. Right now, she needed clarity more than anything else. It worked. The fresh air and greenery surrounding her shifted her focus away from the turmoil of her emotions.

A question nagged at the back of her mind. Dante had never stated exactly why it was that the royal couple couldn't attend the trip. Something had to have come up.

She could call the queen herself to find out. But then she'd be subjected to Her Majesty's persuasive efforts. Sierra didn't think she had the patience or nerve for that right now. There was one other person who came to mind.

Someone who happened to be a woman Sierra considered a friend.

Pulling out her cell phone, she clicked on the icon for one of her contacts. Perna answered on the first ring.

After a few pleasantries and general catching up, Sierra had the answer to her question about why the king and queen wouldn't be traveling anytime soon. Her heart sank when she found out.

Perna was still speaking in her ear. "At his age, they say he'd be foolish to attempt such a taxing itinerary given the irregularity of his heartbeat."

Sierra absorbed the news as she made her way to the nearest bench. Her shoes may as well have been made of bricks. "I see."

"We've been trying to keep it quiet until the doctors had some definitive answers about his condition."

"Thanks, Perna. You've been as helpful as I knew you would be."

With that, Sierra hung up and tucked the phone in her jeans pocket. Then she pulled out the card Dante's aide had handed her in the elevator. Releasing a resigned sigh, she began to dial.

CHAPTER TWO

Three weeks later

SIERRA SHUT HER suitcase and tucked it away in the vast closet in the corner of her even vaster room. The last time she was here at Castle Angilera had seemed like another lifetime. It felt odd to be here again. Which made no sense. She'd spent countless days here as a child. She and Dante running through the miles of hallways, playing hide-and-seek for hours in any of the numerous royal gardens. This castle had been like a second home to her while growing up. So why did she feel like a stranger here now? How had things changed so much in her life that the familiar now felt odd?

Three knocks on the door jostled her out of her reverie.

She didn't need more than one guess to know that it was Dante. He always knocked three times, a slight hesitation just before the third.

Funny how little details such as that one could remain lodged in one's memory. But then, she had several memories of Dante, some prone to rising to the surface at the most inopportune times. Sierra sighed. Looked like she would be adding more to her collection given the trip they were about to take together.

"Come in."

He strode into the room to stand before her. Sierra thought her knees might buckle at the sight of him. He must have been returning from some sort of ceremonial event. He wore a formal, fitted suit jacket with the crest of the house of Angilera on one side of his chest while the coat of arms adorned the other. A slew of honor ribbons sat below the crest.

"Glad to see you've made it. Sorry I wasn't there to greet you. I had a swearing-in ceremony for a new minister."

"How is your father?" she asked, pulling her focus away from the way he looked in his formal attire.

"There has been no change. Which is both good news and bad."

"You should have told me that first day you flew to New York. About his condition."

He stepped farther into the room, leveled a steady gaze on her with those steel gray eyes that were all too easy for a woman to lose herself in. "I didn't want the knowledge to sway your decision about coming. Didn't want any kind of guilt to play a part. I was hoping I could convince you in other ways."

Was it her imagination, or had his voice grown deeper as he finished his words? If he meant any kind of double entendre with the way he ended that sentence, she wasn't about to follow that path.

"My change of heart had more to do with concern for my godfather than any kind of guilt." Enough concern that she'd pleaded with the head designer at House of Perth to give her leave for several days, then wrangled Camille into sitting for her pet hamster while she was away.

He nodded once. "Be that as it may, I should have guessed you would find a way to discover the whole truth, whether I told you or not."

She wasn't sure how to respond to that, so she ignored it. "So, we leave in two days?"

"Correct. We should reach Valhali by Thursday afternoon."

This was all happening so quickly, so unexpectedly, Sierra was having trouble processing all the details. "Remind me exactly where that is again."

Dante said, "It's a small independent nation in the south of Africa, bordering Botswana. The prime minister and his wife will be there to greet us and take us to the Melekhanna lodge, where we'll be staying."

"Followed by a safari starting the next day," she said.

"Correct again."

Sierra had to admit that a feeling of excitement hummed through her veins. An African safari trip sounded so adventurous and exotic. She'd never thought of herself as the safari type. In fact, she hadn't thought about visiting that part of the world at all. Now that she was about to, she couldn't deny the excitement of it all. Despite the potential for disaster, given the company she'd be traveling with.

Her best option was to do her best to keep a safe distance between her and Dante. Surely they'd be surrounded by others most of the time. It wasn't as if they'd be traipsing the African grasslands by themselves.

"There will be two journalists who work there locally who will be with us from the beginning to chronicle our journey through the game reserve and hopefully lend some more visibility to the cause," Dante told her. "A gaggle of reporters from all over the world will join us a few days later to cover the scheduled news conference and meeting with the local conservationists."

Her excitement turned to trepidation. She wasn't used to being the center of attention. Being in front of a group of journalists with cameras flashing in her face—the thought of it made her stomach queasy. Sure, Dante would be the primary attraction, but she was bound to have at least a few questions thrown her way. What if she made a fool of herself with a stupid answer that made no sense? If only she had some of Rula's savvy. Even when Rula said the wrong thing, she could find a way to charm her way out of any sort of embarrassment. A rush of sadness washed over her. These halls held so many happy memories from her youth. Memories that were all at the forefront now that she was back. How she wished she might be able to turn back time and return to the carefree days spent in this castle with Dante and Rula.

"Penny for your thoughts?" Dante's question pierced through her musings.

She blinked at him, trying to come up with a way to answer. "I was just thinking how much I'm looking forward to seeing your mom and dad again," she said, fibbing. "The last time I was in Nocera…"

She didn't need to finish the sentence. The last time Sierra had been here had been for Rula's funeral service.

"They're looking forward to seeing you as

well. Your visit is all Maman has talked about
for the past several days. Though it's unfortu-
nate that your own parents are out of the country."

Grateful that he'd changed the subject, Sierra
offered a small smile. "I'll see them when they
come to New York for my birthday."

"Next month. The seventh," Dante said.

"You remember?"

He playfully tapped her nose. "I remember
everything, Sierra." The amusement faded from
his eyes and his lips thinned. "All of it, before
everything changed."

Changed it had. When Dante had gone from
being a dear childhood friend to someone akin
to a brother-in-law. But Sierra couldn't deny that
there'd been a slight shift in their relationship
even before his courtship of Rula. Unguarded
moments as they'd both grown older and matured. The way Dante's eyes had lingered on
her the first time he'd seen her in a ball gown
at the king's jubilee soiree. How he'd held her
just a moment longer than he might have the
first time they'd danced together.

"I'll let you get settled," Dante said after several heavy moments of silence. Sierra had to
wonder if his thoughts had traveled down a path
of memories as well.

"See you in a couple hours at dinner."

She watched silently as he turned and walked out of the room, shutting the door softly behind him.

The flight to Botswana three days later took a little over nine hours from Istanbul International Airport, where they'd departed after leaving Nocera. The moment they'd landed, Sierra and Dante had hit both the proverbial and literal road running. Now, they were in a Landcruiser their way out of Botswana, headed toward the Valhali border.

A second SUV trailed behind them carrying two bodyguards and a palace aide.

Sierra glanced over at Dante's profile as he sat in the passenger seat next to her. The man was perpetually tanned, his skin a natural golden hue despite the season. Now, sheeted in a thin layer of dust from the bumpy dirt road, he still somehow looked every bit the royal crown prince and heir to a kingdom. Yet, somehow in a rugged, edgy way.

Wow. She really needed to stop focusing on Dante's looks. Or focusing on the man in general. What was wrong with her anyway? She was in Africa! Plenty to see here, no need to fixate on the handsome, alluring prince she was traveling with.

There she went again. Sierra sighed and

turned her gaze to the road. Their driver was a jovial young man who frequently turned to give them friendly smiles as he drove. He'd introduced himself as Banti when he'd picked them up from the airport.

"We'll be there in no time," he said over his shoulder in a charming accent. It never ceased to amaze her, throughout her travels, how so much of the world was fluently bilingual, English flowing smoothly from the lips of many people no matter where she was.

Rula had been fluent in three different languages. Her best friend had always said any queen worth her salt should be bilingual at the least. She'd been determined since barely past her toddler years to marry into the royal family, with no small amount of influence from her ambitious parents, and had worked steadily toward that end.

It had all gone so horribly wrong.

Sierra had wondered more than once over the years if Rula might have chosen a different path had it not been for the urging of her mother and father to aspire to become queen. How different might her life have been?

"What's the matter?" Dante's voice asked above the loud rumbling of tires over rugged road. He'd always been very in tune to her moods.

"Is the ride too rough? I can ask him to pull over for a bit."

She shook her head. "No. I'm fine. Really."

He didn't look convinced.

"Seriously," she began. "Don't worry about—" But she couldn't get the words out as particularly drastic jolt threw her first against the door than hurtled her in Dante's direction. The next thing she knew, she was practically sprawled in his lap. His arms immediately wrapped around her shoulders to hold her steady.

Stunned, she could only stare up at his face. His eyes were shielded behind a pair of aviator sunglasses, but there was no doubt about the tension in his features. It took several moments for Sierra to find her breath.

"I'm so sorry." But when she made an effort to pull away, his arms remained locked around her.

He was silent for several beats before speaking. "Don't be."

Despite the rumbling of the vehicle, despite the dust kicking up around them, Earth might as well have stopped turning. Sierra continued to stare at Dante, knowing full well that she should have moved off his lap already. But she felt dazed and disoriented. Every cell in her body screamed at her to stay where she was and enjoy the scenery with his arms wrapped tightly around her, safe and secure in his embrace despite the treacherous, bouncy ride. Being this close to Dante, having him hold her, feeling his warmth against her skin felt right in a way that she had yet to experience with any other man.

Sierra squeezed her eyes shut and shook her head against the wayward thoughts. Finally, common sense somehow intervened. Forcing her muscles to work, she gave him a tight smile and removed herself from his lap.

"Border checkpoint," the driver announced from the front seat. "This shouldn't take long. No need to be nervous," he added.

Well, it hadn't occurred to her to be nervous until he'd just told her not to. Her anxiety kicked up a notch as their vehicle slowed and several armed soldiers approached. Dante reached for her hand, gave it a reassuring squeeze in his own. The warmth of his palm on hers lowered her anxiety several notches. Their driver exchanged several words with the man who appeared to be in charge of the group. Clearly these men had no idea a foreign crown prince was in the back seat. The lack of fanfare and the bluster finally made sense. Dante was much better off pretending to be an ordinary tourist on an outing with his girlfriend or wife at this stage of their journey. The time for fanfare and publicity would come later.

Sierra gave herself a mental whack at the dangerous word. *Wife*. Lord, she had to find a way to control her thoughts and keep from wandering into such perilous territory.

Their driver was right, with a cursory glance at the paperwork, followed by a pointed look at her and Dante holding hands, the soldier gave them a nod and motioned them to move forward.

They'd driven about a half mile when Banti slowed the vehicle and pulled off to the side.

"Why are we stopping?" Dante asked.

At the exact same moment Sierra said, "Is something wrong?"

"We are in my country now," Banti answered, shooting them a wide grin over his shoulder. "Beautiful Valhali. We can do as we want. Would either of you like to drive?"

Was he serious?

"Absolutely not," she answered automatically. She'd learned how to drive a vehicle on her fifteenth birthday, but had never really had need to drive herself anywhere. And since moving to New York, the subway had been her main mode of transportation.

Dante however was already hopping out of the vehicle, a look of clear excitement on his face. "You bet I do." He glanced behind him over his shoulder. "But we have to hurry before

Otto and the others catch up to play the body-guard card to try to stop me."

He was in the driver's seat in the next moment. Banti extended his hand to her, opening her door. "Would you like to go sit in the front by your—"

Sierra didn't let him finish the sentence.

"Sure. Why not?" Though her heart was hammering in her rib cage at the prospect.

Dante seemed to be enjoying himself when he took the wheel. The expression on his face could only be described as one of pure glee. She pressed her back against the seat and braced herself as he pressed the accelerator. The Landcruiser surged forward, and soon Dante was driving over the rough terrain like he'd been driving in this country his whole life.

The second car finally caught up and pulled along beside them. The two men in the passenger seats shook their heads at the prince as if chastising a child. Dante merely shrugged and grinned back at them. A wave of nostalgia washed over Sierra at the sight. The moment reminded her so much of Dante as a preteen when he'd sneak off to meet her and Rula at the beach or to simply get away from the castle.

"Thanks, Sierra," he said with a grin as he assisted her out of the front passenger seat.

Sierra blinked at him in confusion. What was

he thanking her for? "Banti's the one who let you drive."

"I just mean thanks for being a good sport and not arguing how dangerous and reckless I was being by driving."

His statement took her aback. She had the distinct impression arguing with him about driving would have been exactly what Rula would have done. Her emotions were in enough turmoil without the knowledge that Dante might be comparing her to her lost friend.

Heaven knew she did enough of that herself. And she always came up short.

The sense of exhilaration Dante had felt while driving hadn't abated even a fraction as they approached their lodge two hours later. Banti had no idea how much of a favor he'd done for him with such a seemingly innocuous offer. No way would Dante have been allowed such an indulgence if his parents or anyone else from the royal court were here. Too risky. He was the sole heir. He couldn't be so reckless with his health and safety. He had no doubt he was going to get an earful from Otto and the aide at some point. But he'd worry about that later when the time came.

He'd expected Sierra to protest as well. But she'd taken it in stride, hadn't said a word against it once he'd accepted Banti's offer to let him drive.

Rula would have no doubt done the exact opposite. He could hear his former wife's voice in his head. *Don't even consider it, Dante. You're in a foreign country, in a completely remote area. Help could be hours away if something were to happen.*

By contrast, Sierra had clearly been nervous, but she'd still jumped into the passenger seat next to him. He could still hear her excited laughter as he took a particularly sharp turn in the road a little too fast. She may not have liked it, but she'd let Dante make the decision. And she'd trusted him once he had. To this day, even after all this time having known them both, it still struck him how different the two women had been despite being so close.

Dante gave his head a brisk shake. Try as he might, he couldn't seem to keep mentally comparing Sierra to his deceased wife, right or wrong.

He released a deep sigh. *Wrong.* Of course, it was completely wrong.

Dante stole a glance at her as they pulled up in front of the lodge. Her cheeks were glowing a rosy red, from both the sun and exertion of their ride, he would guess. She'd been chewing on her bottom lip, rendering it swollen and crimson.

She'd kept applying some kind of balm to them during the drive. Every time she'd uncapped it, the scent of berries had wafted through the air. What might that taste like if he were to taste it on her lips?

Whoa.

Dante pulled up short. Now his thoughts were leading him into perilously dangerous territory. Sierra was a family friend, here with him only as a dignitary. Dante absolutely couldn't lose sight of either of those facts.

So instead of opening her door and helping her out of the vehicle when they'd come to a stop, he let Banti do it instead. Then he forced himself not to so much as look in her direction.

"The prime minister with his wife and their group will be here in a few hours," Banti informed them. "They wanted to give you both a chance to settle in and freshen up before their arrival."

Sierra's shoulders dropped, a look of relief washed over her features. She was clearly relieved at the news. Dante wanted to kick himself. He hadn't even considered how new this all must be for her. She was no seasoned royal on her latest state sponsored trip. She hadn't even been rehearsed on exactly how to behave or what to expect, aside from a brief consultation with his *maman* after her arrival in Nocera.

He was going to have to do his best to guide her, and to reassure her along the way. He had no doubt she was going to be an amazingly impressive representative of his kingdom. She just had to believe it too.

He knew how much he and his parents were asking of her. It spoke to her character that she was even here in the first place to help them out. Not to mention the heavy shadow of the past that would follow them. He would have to find a way to truly thank her for all that she was doing for the sake of the Crown and this trip. Not that he had any idea what he might do for her. Sierra had always been an independent soul. She'd gone after her dream of pursuing a career in fashion and was unsurprisingly successful in one of the most competitive markets in the world. She hardly needed anything from him.

"Come, follow me." Banti broke into his thoughts, motioning them toward the lodge. The Melekhanna lodge could have made a perfect picture for an article about Valhali in a travel magazine.

The structure appeared more luxurious than Dante might have guessed. Lanterns adorned the perimeter of a wide porch that wrapped around the entire structure. Individual egg-shaped hammocks hung from either side of the wide entryway. Comfortable looking wicker furniture with thick colorful cushions adorned the patio just outside the wooden porch steps. The thatched roof was the color of dark reed, blending in well with the surroundings, as if the lodge was part of the natural environment and not a man-made structure with all the comforts of a grand resort inside.

Sierra appeared to be studying the building with awe as Banti led them up the wooden steps. "Wow," she uttered on a breathless whisper.

"It's pretty impressive."

She nodded. "It certainly is." She continued to take in her surroundings before adding, "I have to admit. I had no idea what to expect when I agreed to come here. So far, I've been impressed at every turn."

Her words sent a surge of pleasure rushing through him. "There's so much more left to see."

She chuckled with what might have been delight. "I can't wait."

Dante checked his gold and onyx watch for the umpteenth time and wondered if somehow it was actually malfunctioning. Or else it meant time was moving unbearably slowly. After a lengthy email to his parents assuring them their arrival had gone smoothly, followed by a long shower, he was more than anxious to proceed with the evening. Today was the first day he could remember in a long time that he'd actually felt…something, anything. Now, he was itching to get back out there. After Rula's death, he'd spent several weeks in a state of numbness. The people of his kingdom referred to him as the Ever Grieving Prince. But no one knew the whole truth. Not even his parents. It was hard to grieve a marriage that had never really felt genuine. He had loved Rula. And he knew she'd loved him, in her own way.

But he wasn't naive enough to believe either of them had ever been *in* love with each other. Rula had wanted to be a queen. And Dante had been her means to that end. Rula had wanted the title. It just so happened that she needed a husband who was a crown prince to achieve it. It had cost her everything, her very life. He knew he bore some of the responsibility for his wife's untimely death. Perhaps if he had tried harder, attempted to be more affectionate, things might have turned out differently.

He'd thought from the beginning that Rula understood theirs was to be a marriage of convenience, not one based on love or affection. How tragically mistaken he'd been. Rula clearly had needed more from him. Ultimately, he'd been unable to give her what she might have wanted most—a spouse who could have indeed loved her.

As the heir, Dante would have to remarry eventually. This time, he'd be better prepared. He'd make sure his next wife knew exactly what to expect from their marriage. He'd make sure that she understood the union would be barely more than a business arrangement. A marriage of convenience to ensure the stability of the kingdom and produce the next heirs.

The lady would have to understand and agree that she couldn't expect anything more from him, least of all any kind of true affection or love.

He scoffed at the very notion. People like him couldn't afford such emotion.

Dante swore, rubbed his forehead. This was useless. Why was he standing here in his room, thinking thoughts about what might have been? None of it made any difference whatsoever. Nothing would change the past now. He'd failed his wife. He would have to go to his own grave with the guilt of that knowledge.

Sierra had never actually come out and said so. But he knew she blamed him for her dear friend's fate as well. At least partially. The two women were as close as sisters. Of course she would hold him partly responsible. It only made sense. If there was any way to atone himself in her eyes, he had to be able to find a way to do so. And that was why he hadn't fought harder to dissuade his mother from asking her on this trip. To give him some time with her, to try to convince her to forgive him somehow. Maybe it was selfish of him, but he couldn't spend the rest of his life knowing Sierra Compari might never forgive him for his greatest mistake. Though he could hardly blame her.

For now, he needed some air. Enough of the melancholy thoughts tormenting his mind. Yanking open the door, he strode out onto the shared porch and toward the front of the lodge. Two things struck him at once. The color of the sky as the sun was beginning to set. And that Sierra was outside as well, just a few feet away on the patio. She sat in one of the eggshell hammocks, scribbling furiously in a sketchbook spread open on her lap.

Dante nearly turned around so as not to disturb whatever she was in the middle of. She had her bottom lip between her teeth, her bare feet dangling. Her hair was still damp from her shower, haphazardly tied up in a knot at her neck. Soft, delicate curls framed her face. She'd changed into a calf-length skirt and a white collared top that barely reached the waistband of the skirt. She fit into the picture before him perfectly, as if she belonged here, under the darkening African sky.

She must have sensed his presence. She didn't

bother to look away from her page when she spoke to him.

"I'm afraid my colored pencils don't do the scene any justice," she said softly, still sketching. "And there's no way to capture this on a cell phone camera."

He moved closer, pulled up the nearby cushioned wicker chair and sat down. "It is rather striking." The sky was a deep crimson over the grasslands, waves of clouds reaching the horizon. Dante felt as if he'd stepped into a life-size painting.

"Breathtaking," Sierra answered, looking up briefly before putting pencil to paper once more.

"Are you sketching the sunset?"

She shook her head. "I'm sketching a jumpsuit. Something a woman might wear to a casual cocktail party. Or to Sunday brunch. I've decided the pant legs will be loose and flowing. Slightly pleated, like the pattern of those clouds. I can only hope to find a fabric that comes even close to that shade of red back in New York."

Dante couldn't find the words with which to respond. He'd never seen this Sierra before, not even when they were kids. Sierra at work was a novel sight. Totally focused, her right hand moving furiously over the page, eyebrows drawn in concentration. He knew she was passionate about her work. She'd left her home and moved halfway across the world in its pursuit, after all. But he'd never actually seen her create before. It was a sight to behold. Once again, he felt as if he might be intruding on a private moment and almost rose to leave.

It was as if she'd read his mind, something she'd always been rather good at. "You don't have to go," she told him. "I'm almost done."

Moments later, she tucked the last pencil into a thin silver case and dropped it into a canvas bag near her feet. Before she could close the cover on her sketch, he rose and reached her side. "May I?" he asked, gesturing to the book in her hand, genuinely curious.

A tightening of her lips, a slight hesitation, but she turned the sketchbook around and pushed it toward him. Dante would be hard-pressed to describe what he was looking at. Somehow, she'd captured the visual magnificence of the scene before them and transferred it into the design of an article of clothing. And she'd done so with nothing but blank paper and colored pencils. Plus her imagination.

"Wow," was all he could think of to say.

She tilted her head. "Is that a good 'wow' or a bad 'wow'?"

She had to ask? "Definitely the former. I don't know much about women's clothing, but what you've captured here is beyond impressive."

Her shoulders dropped, and she cast him a small smile. "Thanks. I'm really happy to hear that. To be honest, I surprised myself. I've had a bit of a rough patch coming up with new ideas lately. And then I came out here and saw this." She gestured in the general direction of the horizon. "I had to sit down and try to see where it led."

Dante glanced down at the image once more. He'd have to say it had led her well.

CHAPTER THREE

SIERRA COULDN'T HELP the rush of giddiness that flashed through her at Dante's compliment. How silly of her. After all, it was true what he said. He didn't really know anything about women's clothing. His opinion on her design shouldn't mean anything to her.

But it did. It meant more than she would have liked it to.

Now, he pointed to her drawing. "Do ideas such as this one just come to you?" he asked. "Out of nowhere?"

Sierra scoffed. If only that were the case. "Hardly. This trip might be just what I needed."

"A creative jolt," he said.

She held her right hand up, crossed her fingers. "Let's hope."

"Well, if this is any indication, I'd say you're off to a good start."

Sierra hadn't wanted to show him what she'd drawn. Given his reaction, she was glad she had. She'd sensed his presence the moment he'd stepped out of his doorway, had had a fleeting urge to flee before he could reach her side. But that was childish. She could hardly go running every time he appeared. They'd be spending several days in each other's company. Which left only one other option—she would have to try to clamp down on the inconvenient awareness of Dante Angilera she couldn't seem to shake despite all the time that had passed. Despite the fact that he was once her best friend's husband. For instance, she should not be noticing how muscular his chest appeared under the soft cotton shirt he wore, nor the way his shirtsleeves were rolled up just above his elbows and how his forearms looked like they may have been sculpted by a master artist.

"It's louder here than I would have thought," she said, by way of conversation, just to have some kind of dialogue and to redirect her focus.

Dante lifted his head, as if listening, then nodded. "I noticed that too. Cicadas humming. Punctuated by the shriek of a monkey in a nearby tree. And birds. Lots of birdsong."

Yet another sound rang from his pocket, this one much more modern. Dante pulled out his phone and glanced at the screen. "From Banti. He's texted both of us."

"I left my phone in the room," she told him.

So that she could focus on what she'd wanted to draw uninterrupted. "What does it say?"

"He wants to let us know that the prime minister and his wife should be here within minutes. They're bringing along a couple of journalists. We'll be meeting them outside the lobby. Followed by dinner then an evening full of activities and entertainment."

Sierra jumped off her seat with a resigned sigh. It all sounded so exhausting. It was during moments like this that she wished she could have been more like Rula. A stab of guilt seared through her center. Rula should have been the one here in her stead.

Rula was the consummate dignitary who always knew how to present herself and exactly what to say and how to behave. Just as a future queen should. Sierra would much rather stay here enjoying the ever-changing scenery and the solitude. If she had her way, she might spread a blanket in the field, grab a sandwich and a bottle of wine, and simply sit out here to enjoy the view, watching the changing sky. But the vision her mind concocted at those thoughts didn't have her sitting on that blanket alone. Dante was next to her, pouring that wine and they were sharing that sandwich.

Stop.

"Guess we better make our way down there then."

To her surprise, he reached out and gently grasped her elbow. "Just another minute."

Huh. Maybe she wasn't the only one trying to overcome an introverted nature. It must be so much harder for Dante if that were the case. A prince didn't have much choice about socializing, did he? His whole life centered around meetings with other prominent people and public appearances. A life she couldn't imagine. Unlike Rula, who had wanted nothing more out of her own life.

"I just want to enjoy this a bit longer." He gestured generally around him. "Once the prime minister and his entourage get here, moments like this will be hard to come by."

That sounded fine by her, to enjoy the peace until the very last second. So they simply stood side by side in silence, with nature providing plenty of background noise. The sun continued its slow descent. The rushing water of a nearby river competed with the hum of the cicadas. Her fingers itched to reach for her sketchbook again, more ideas rushing through her mind. But it would have to wait, of course.

Sure enough, the moment didn't last long. A commotion of noise could be heard in the distance, clouds of dust rising in the air a few meters to the right of the lodge. The other guests were arriving.

Dante tilted his head, gave her a defeated look, then motioned for her toward the steps.

Time zero. Help me out here, Rula. So that I don't somehow say the wrong thing or act the wrong way, Sierra pleaded to her lost friend.

Though she knew she had no right to ask.

Dressed in traditional attire complete with head-dresses and beaded neck chains, the prime minister and his wife looked regal and ceremonious when they exited their vehicles.

To her relief, they both set Sierra immediately at ease with their friendly introductions and smiling faces. For his part, Dante appeared equally cordial. He may have been hesitant and less than enthusiastic earlier about the festivities starting, but Sierra saw now that he was in his element. He introduced her as Lady Sierra, a family friend who would be accompanying him.

They all insisted on the use of their first names.

Nantu, the prime minister, threw a hand over Dante's shoulder, his mouth tightening in a solemn line. "Again, I want to convey in person our deepest condolences on the loss of the princess," he said to Dante, gesturing to his wife.

"We were both so saddened when we heard," he added.

"Thank you, Your Honor."

"Call me Nantu, remember?" he reminded Dante.

"And thank you for the flowers you had sent all the way from Valhali. It was a beautiful arrangement that brightened up the palace during its darkest days. The lilies were particularly vibrant."

Of course, Dante would remember such a detail, Sierra thought. Or he'd made sure to look it up before embarking on the trip. Such a thing would not have even occurred to her.

"You're welcome, my friend," Nantu said.

It was then Sierra noticed the two individuals hovering on the outskirts of the circle. A strawberry-red-haired woman and a balding, older gentleman. They were both clad in western clothing. The man was furiously snapping photos with a complicated looking camera. The woman was tapping furiously away at her phone screen.

Two of the journalists who were here to ensure this trip got the publicity the queen was after for her foundation. Sierra wondered when the rest of the crew would arrive. Probably not long now.

The prime minister's wife, Kaliha, approached

her. "You'll get used to them being around," she told Sierra, her singsong voice laced with a charming accent. "After a while, they just blend into the background."

Sierra wanted to believe her. But just at that moment, she noticed the camera was pointed in her direction. The reporter clicked several snaps in rapid succession. Sierra did her best to summon a smile, but it wasn't easy. She was used to being surrounded by lenses, but she was never the one in the frame. The models she worked with were the usual targets.

"I'm going to vehemently hope you're right," she said, not believing the statement for one moment. How could one get used to constantly having their photo taken as they went about their activities? A glance at Dante gave her a clue. He seemed completely at ease as the camera turned on him and the reporter snapped away.

"Come, let's get acquainted," Kaliha said, leading her away a few feet away from the action. Why did Sierra get the feeling the distance was for her own benefit and not for Kaliha? Heavens, she must look as out of place as she felt.

"And we can give those two a chance to catch up," Kaliha stated once they'd moved out of earshot, glancing in the direction where the men stood chatting. They gave every appearance of being longtime friends.

"Has your husband known Dante long?" Sierra asked, genuinely curious despite herself.

"They met a few years back at a UN summit and hit it off. Nantu has spoken fondly of him ever since."

No surprise there, Sierra thought. Most people found Dante charming and good-natured, both men and women. Particularly women.

"It's nice to see the prince finally traveling, even if it's in an official capacity," the other woman added after a beat, her gaze still locked on where Dante stood with her husband. "I know the loss of his wife hit him hard. And it's nice that he has someone like you to keep him company."

Sierra immediately shook her head. It was important to make sure no one got any false impressions of what she was doing here. Especially given the presence of all sorts of journalists and photographers. This could turn into a situation ripe for the spread of false rumors. She didn't need that complication in her life right now. And neither did Dante. "Oh, it's not— I'm his former— He used to be marr—" She stopped her sputtering to suck in a deep breath. Why in the world had she lost the ability to speak all of a sudden? "I'm only here as a representative of Nocera and the royal family," she explained, doing her best to keep her voice steady.

Kaliha tilted her head to the side. "I know that, dear," the other woman answered with a small but rather mischievous smile. "My point still stands."

Before Sierra could find a way to respond, Kaliha patted her hand. "Tell me about yourself, dear. Is this your first time in Africa?"

The tension in her midsection loosened a fraction at the change of topic. "Yes, it is. I'm terribly excited to be here. It's already given me a creative nudge, so to speak."

Even as she sat here, her creative juices were flowing. The darkening sky dotted with twinkling lights, the exotic caw of a bird in the distance, a soft breeze that carried with it the scent of the colorful flowers planted by the patio. Her senses were in heaven.

Kaliha's eyebrows lifted half an inch. "Oh? How so?"

Sierra explained what she did back in New York, the difficulties she'd been having coming up with new ideas, and how inspiring she'd found the sunset earlier. To her surprise, her words flowed freely and comfortably. She'd just met the woman, but something about her warm personality had Sierra completely at ease. As if she were speaking with an old friend and not the spouse of the leader of a sovereign nation. On the surface, she had nothing in common with this woman. But she felt as if she might have made a new friend.

Their conversation was cut short with the arrival of Banti, who announced that their meal was ready to be served. Within seconds, the prime minister was at Kalihi's side offering her his arm.

Dante followed suit, holding his hand out to Sierra. She took it, a tingle of electricity spreading along her skin at the contact. Dante's fingers wrapped around her wrist gently, his eyes lingered on hers for a loaded second. The sound of a camera snapping a photo echoed in the distance.

Dante guided Sierra to where Banti was leading them, a long wooden table by the front patio of the lodge. In the center sat a cornucopia of fruits, sandwiches, sliced vegetables. Each plate looked exotic and different, arranged aesthetically. The vivid colors reminded him of paintings he'd seen in some of the world's most renowned museums.

"I don't even recognize some of these fruits," Sierra said as he pulled out her chair and she sat down. He planted himself in the one next to her once the prime minister and his wife found their own chairs. Tall, lit candles atop the table accented the various dishes. Lanterns hung from poles staked in the ground at each corner.

"Looks like we'll be dining under the stars." He was about to add how romantic the scene was but thought better of it. He couldn't remember the last time he'd eaten dinner outside in the company of a beautiful and charming woman.

Whoa.

It was exactly those kinds of thoughts that he had to avoid. Never mind that the whole setting he found himself in was quite romantic indeed. The soft candlelight cast a soft glow on Sierra's rosy cheeks. The sparkling silver bright stars in the velvet dark sky above. The hum of the cicadas echoing in the air around them. A myriad of unfamiliar scents mingled with the nostalgia of the vanilla rose combination he associated with Sierra. He would have to ignore all that.

Exactly when had he become so poetic anyway? This was essentially a state sponsored dinner. With journalists dining along with them for heaven's sake. There shouldn't be anything remotely intimate about it. Determined to consistently remind himself of those facts, Dante reached for the bowl closest to him, thinly sliced cucumbers dotted with marinated olives, then offered it to Sierra. Nantu and his wife had already spooned an assortment of items onto their own plates.

A server wearing a bright headscarf that matched her dress appeared between their chairs to pour them a ruby red wine. Dante recognized the label as one of the finest vintages from a well-known South African vineyard. Another immediately followed in her wake with a tray of gooey vegetable lasagna and spooned generous portion for each of them.

"This looks and smells divine," Sierra stated, taking a small bit of the steaming pasta. She practically purred with pleasure and Dante found himself having to look away.

Across the table, Nantu lifted his glass in a toast. Grateful for the distraction, Dante followed suit. Sierra lifted her glass then took a hesitant, small sip of wine. Her eyes grew wide with pleasure as she swallowed.

She held the glass out at eye level, seemingly studying it.

"I take it you like it?" he asked.

"It's like nectar from heaven. And the color is so strikingly robust. It kind of reminds me of the sky earlier as the sun was setting."

Dante couldn't help but feel a twinge of envy. Sierra's world seemed to be so vibrant, full of color. She truly took note of everything around her and appreciated the world's beauty unlike anyone he'd ever met. By contrast, most days he felt as if he were sleepwalking through his day. Saying all the right things, meeting with all the right people, providing a royal spokesman with all the right quotes. Even the events he did for charity seemed hollow at times. He wasn't the one usually doing all the work. Just a symbol of the Crown. Nothing more.

Get a grip.

He was perilously close to "the poor prince" territory here, with such self-pitying thoughts. As a distraction, he picked up the wine bottle and topped off both their glasses.

Sierra held a hand up before he'd reached close to the top of the rim. "Whoa. As good as that is, I should probably slow it down a bit."

"Fair point. It has been a rather long day." He should probably take it easy on the wine as well. "But what's done is done." He couldn't very well pour it back in the bottle.

She nodded slowly, a sly smile over her lips. "I supposed it would be a shame to waste such delicious wine."

"It certainly would," he agreed, tapping his glass to hers as gently as possible. It was rather full.

"The reporters look awfully busy," Sierra commented as they polished off the salads and the main course. "Even as they eat, they're scribbling away on their little notepads."

"At least they're here to do a job."

She lifted an eyebrow. "Meaning?"

He hadn't intended for his inner thoughts from earlier to rise so close to the surface. "Never mind. It's not important."

She set her fork down. "Tell me," she prodded.

Dante did his best to explain his meaning. It was hard to put into words but if there was anyone he'd try to do it for, it was Sierra. "What value am I providing here exactly?" he asked. "I'm not one of the conservationists. I don't take care of the animals. I'm just here as a mouthpiece. A figurehead."

Sierra's mouth fell open. "You can't believe that, Dante."

"It's the truth, isn't it?"

She turned in her seat to face him directly. "On the contrary, Dante. What you're doing here is very important. Drawing attention to animal and environmental conservation is more crucial now than ever before. So many species are close to extinction. And the way some of these animals are hunted for profit is an absolute crime."

She was right about that. "An international crime," he agreed. "Yet it keeps happening." But what was he doing about any of it? Aside from speaking about it and spending time at a safari lodge? "It's not the cause I'm questioning," he told her, once again surprising himself with the revelation.

"I don't know what that means," Sierra answered after a pause. "But it's people like you that others pay attention to."

Leave it to Sierra to find a way to make him feel better about his mostly ceremonial role. Not that he was surprised. She'd always been one of the few people in his orbit who knew exactly understood his insecurities about becoming the leader his people needed. And she always knew what to say to smooth those insecurities over. Saints above, how he'd missed that. Dante hadn't even realized just how badly until this moment.

He didn't have a chance to respond as the server who had earlier brought the wine rolled a tray cart full of pastries and cakes up to the table beside them.

"Something sweet, madam? Sir?"

Sierra began to shake her head then leaned closer to the cart. "As full as I am, I don't think I can pass up on that banana cake."

The woman sliced a thick slice and drizzled a bronze glaze over the piece with a flourish before placing it in front of Sierra.

Some of the drizzle dropped onto her lips as she took a bite, and it took every ounce of his will not to reach over and wipe it away with his thumb.

He clenched his fist around his wineglass instead. It was a wonder the stem didn't snap.

CHAPTER FOUR

SIERRA'S SENSES WERE on overload. It had to be the exhaustion. Dante was right, it had been a rather long day. And this meal was much richer than her usual nightly fare—a quick bite from a food truck on her way home or a boxed meal heated in the microwave. But she couldn't blame either of those things for the way her heart was thudding in her chest. Or for the heady feeling fluttering in the pit of her stomach. No. That had everything to do with the man sitting next to her. Despite the slew of people around them, Sierra and Dante may as well have been alone. Her focus was zeroed in on him so completely. She couldn't seem to help herself.

Everything about this night was downright magical—dinner under a clear African sky dotted with bright stars, the humming nature sounds all around them, the sound of the flowing river in the distance. The mouthwatering food. Not to mention the delicious wine.

No wonder she was forgetting herself. She barely had any kind of social life with her busy schedule, couldn't even recall the last time she'd had a date. Now all this activity was throwing her off. She'd probably have the same reaction to any red-blooded male under the same circumstances.

Right. A voice inside her head mocked her. She wasn't fooling herself.

As if she could ignore the history she and Dante had together. As if she'd forget all the times she'd felt a pang of longing when he was near, even after his engagement to her best friend had been announced.

It was all so wrong.

"Sierra? Did you hear me?" Dante's voice broke into her thoughts. He was rising out of his chair with his hand extended to her.

"I'm sorry?"

He gave her an indulgent smile. "I said the entertainment is about to start. The lodge staffers have arranged for a customary dance ceremony to welcome us here."

Sierra stood and they followed Banti and the others to a makeshift stage on the patio at the back of the lodge. A small bonfire burned several feet away. Just as they took their seats, the beat of rhythmic drums began to flow through the air. A group of people appeared from the side of the building, four women and four men. The ladies wore long woven skirts with lacey, brightly colored tops. The men had on leather ankle-length pants and white tops. All wore crowns of beads atop their heads.

Sierra watched, mesmerized, as they began stomping their feet and dancing around the fire, perfectly in sync and perfectly in tune to the music. Her eyes moved from the dancers to the bonfire. It was as if the flames had become a part of the dance, flickering and moving along with the humans performing around it. She'd never seen anything like it, and would remember the vision for the rest of her days.

After a few minutes, a different beat began to play. Slower this time, the movements of the dancers shifted in response. The men bowed before the women, their hands clasped behind their backs. The women continued to dance, circling the men then circling the fire.

After several moments the drumbeat stopped and the dancers faced them, then bowed to the audience.

Sierra felt as if she'd experienced a masterpiece performance. Belatedly, she realized everyone else had started clapping. While she'd been sitting there stunned by the beauty and wonder of what she'd just witnessed.

One of the dancers approached her, as another went over to where Kaliha and Nantu sat.

"Come, my lady," she said, reaching for her hand. "I will show you how." She turned her focus on Dante. "You too, sir."

Sierra immediately started to protest. She'd always had two left feet. Rula had been the graceful, coordinated one of the two of them. Rula had been the one who'd attended all the ballet classes and who'd taken voice lessons, while Sierra could often be found swinging from trees outside their family cottage when she wasn't down by the river sketching in the dirt with a stick.

She was likely to fall on her face if she attempted any of the moves she'd just witnessed. But the woman was not taking no for an answer, her smile encouraging. She gave Sierra an enthusiastic nod. And Dante had already stood and was looking at her expectantly. He couldn't be serious. He knew her better than to think she should really attempt this.

Apparently not. "Come on, Sierra. Nantu and Kaliha are already on the dance floor." He tilted his head in their direction. "It will be fun," he added with a smile. The light from the fire cast a halolike glow on his dark hair. The merriment behind his eyes lent a golden light to their depths.

How in the world was she supposed to turn him down when he was smiling at her that way?

With more than a little trepidation, Sierra stood and the two of them followed the dancer to the bonfire, where Nantu and Kaliha were mimicking the movements she'd just witnessed. They clearly didn't need any kind of lesson and appeared to be pros who done this more than once before. Sierra felt like the uncoordinated nerd at the high school dance, the one so desperately trying to fit in and praying that no one was paying any attention to her. But that was fallacy, of course. Dante's eyes were focused squarely in her direction.

His unwavering attention was only making this harder for her.

The dancer took Sierra's hand in hers and Dante's in the other. "Like this," she said, first stomping her right foot twice, then the left one once. Then she repeated the action. Okay. That seemed simple enough. Sierra copied her movements. Then she did it again. Dante didn't even appear to be trying. He was just stomping the dirt indiscriminately. Somehow, he still appeared to be in tune with the beat and the other dancers.

"That's great, my lady!" the dancer exclaimed. "Now just make it faster."

Sierra tried…she really did. But as soon as

she attempted the faster pace, her one foot got caught in the hem of her skirt. Her other foot only caught air as she tried to balance herself. There was nothing for it, she was about to go down. A shriek of alarm tore from her lips as her mind registered how close she was to the bonfire.

But a pair of steady hands grabbed her about the waist before she could topple.

And Dante was there, to stop her from falling into the flames.

Yet Sierra still got the feeling she'd been saved from one fire only to land in another.

The relief that she hadn't fallen flat on her face was immediately replaced by something else. Dante was holding her, his arms tight around her middle, his breath hot against her cheek. Sierra lost all sense of the here and now. She could only zero in on the sensations coursing through her core. The feel of his arms around her, the heat of his body against her body, his warm breath against her cheek.

"Steady there, I have you."

Heaven help her, the images and thoughts those words invoked had her pulse skyrocketing, already high from the adrenaline resulting from her near fall.

She looked up to glance at his face. Reassuring, protective…handsome, so devastatingly handsome. Her gaze dropped to his lips. Like so many times in the past, she wondered what it would feel like to kiss him, to brush his lips with hers. What would he taste like? Would he still have traces of the ruby rich wine they'd shared earlier? Some of the dessert he'd indulged in?

If only they were just two ordinary people. If only he hadn't been married to her closest friend who'd so tragically been lost. If only he wasn't the crown prince of her homeland.

But the reality was that Dante was heir to a kingdom. Someone like her would simply be a distraction who provided little to no value to someone like him. Unlike Rula, she hadn't been prepared or trained to be a royal in any sense. Dante deserved someone by his side who had done just that. But it was hard to remember all that in this moment, with Dante's eyes dark and focused on her face.

Sierra wasn't sure how much time passed, with her simply standing in his embrace, before Kaliha appeared at her side. "Are you all right, dear?"

Sierra nodded, straightening and stepping out of Dante's grasp. Was it her imagination or did his hands just tighten around her midsection ever so slightly when she'd begun to remove herself?

"Yes, yes, I'm fine. Just a bit of a klutz."

Kaliha's gaze darted from her face to Dante's and back again. "Well, how fortunate that the prince moved so quickly. You were in good hands."

"Quite literally," Sierra said with a small chuckle, trying to make light of things, as lame an attempt as it was. To her horror, she looked around to find every eye trained solely on her. "I'm sorry to have alarmed everyone. I'm fine, really. Just not as dexterous as you clearly are."

Kaliha patted her arm. "I grew up doing these dances. You'll get the hang of it."

Ha! As if she'd ever try again. "Thank you," was all she could come up to say.

Sierra resisted the urge to groan out loud and watched Kaliha return to her husband's side. Just as she'd predicted, she'd just made a complete fool of herself. In front of the prime minister and his wife, no less. Not to mention the lodge staff and the two reporters. Great. There would probably be color photos of her in the papers and online tomorrow tripping over her own feet.

"I'm so sorr—" the dancer began.

Sierra held up a hand to stop her. "Please,

don't apologize. The fault lies solely with me and my two left feet."

The woman gave her a grateful nod before turning away to find a more promising candidate to teach.

Sierra turned to find Dante watching her. "Uh… I should be thanking you too, of course. My first night here and it could have been a disastrous one. I imagine a game drive would be tough to do with a broken leg."

He shrugged. "Don't mention it. And for the record, you were doing fine until…well, until you weren't."

She cringed. It was an obvious attempt at trying to make her feel better. Which she appreciated but wasn't falling for.

"I think I'm done on the dance floor," she told him. "I'm sure you'd be able to find another partner, one who's a bit more dexterous, hopefully." For one, the female journalist was eyeing him from across the bonfire with clear interest.

Dante chuckled. "You can't get rid of me that easily." He led her back to the table. "Can I get you some more wine?"

That was the last thing she needed. "Absolutely not," she answered without hesitation. "Actually, I think I'm ready to retire for the night." More than ready. Between all the excitement and the tiredness, she just wanted to crawl under the netted canopy of the four-poster in her room and get some rest. Maybe sleep would help her to sort out the completely inconvenient emotions that had been churning through her gut back there. To imagine kissing Dante, of all things. What had gotten into her?

"I feel bad for leaving without saying good night to Kaliha and the prime minister," she told him.

"I'll explain to them later that you were exhausted and dead on your feet."

"Thanks. And tell them I should have known better than to attempt that dance on the best of days, let alone after a day of travel and all that delicious food. Oh, also there was the cabernet."

"They will understand," he reassured her. "Here, I'll walk you to your room."

Sierra wanted to decline his offer, but there was no tactful way to explain that she needed distance right now, particularly from him. *Especially* from him.

She gritted her teeth to keep from protesting. "Thank you," she said instead, following him up the steps of the lodge then around the corner toward the suite of rooms.

When they reached her door, Dante paused, searching her face for several moments. A heavy silence hung in the air between them. For the life of her, Sierra couldn't think of a thing to say in order to fill it. Even after she'd opened her door and turned back to face him, he hesitated, continuing to linger at the threshold. For a moment, Sierra felt exposed, unguarded. Could he somehow see what had been her thoughts earlier? The way she'd reacted at the feel of his arms around her? Did he somehow guess where her imagination had led about placing her lips on his?

For one insane moment, she was tempted to invite him inside. They were friends after all, weren't they? Nothing wrong with a bit of conversation with an old friend. But she wasn't fooling herself. She wouldn't be inviting him in for a chat. They would both know it. And then what?

Not to mention, everyone still at the bonfire would no doubt notice the prince's absence. The speculation that would follow would run rampant. The journalists in particular would have a field day with the knowledge that the prince had left with his companion and hadn't bothered to return.

No, asking Dante to come inside her room was out of the question.

"Guess we have a big day tomorrow," she said instead, by way of an attempt at conversation.

"Good night, Sierra," was all he said. Then he turned on his heel and walked away.

"Good night, dear prince," she answered, but not until he was well out of earshot.

Dante lingered outside his room, waiting until he heard the click of Sierra's door shutting behind her. For one insane moment, he thought about going back and knocking on her door. And then what? What exactly would he say? That he didn't want the night to end? That he wanted to spend some more time with her because these last few hours in her company had been some of the most enjoyable time he'd spent in much too long? Since even before Rula had passed?

Of course he couldn't tell her any of that. At best he would sound like some character out of a romantic comedy movie delivering a few cheesy lines. At worst he would sound desperate and lonely.

If the shoe fits...

Enough! He needed a distraction. He also needed a shower. Not just to wash away the dust and dirt of the evening but also to clear his mind and try to regain some focus.

He should probably use cold water.

Plus he'd reached the point of tiredness where it would actually be difficult to fall asleep. All these crazy thoughts. His attraction to someone he considered an old friend had to be the result of his exhaustion. There was no other rational explanation.

Sure, he'd had a minor crush on Sierra when they were younger, kids really. But he was an adult now, heir to the throne. He'd been a married man once. Would have to marry again. Papa already regularly nagged him about meeting eligible ladies. Or, to use Papa's term, *suitable young women who may qualify.* Just last week he'd tried to set Dante up with a member of the Swedish royal family. As if his next marriage were some kind of reality game show.

In a way, Dante supposed Papa was right. Weren't there constant bets in the gaming halls of Nocera about when and who he might marry?

Dante's lack of any kind of romantic entanglements only fed fuel to the gossip fire. As well as the people of Nocera, the newspapers also called him the Ever Grieving Prince. He couldn't seem to get over losing his wife, they speculated. He couldn't seem to move on and find another woman to wed. The truth was, Dante had no intention of moving on, knew he didn't deserve any kind of happiness. When the time came, he would marry once again. But this time there'd be no false pretenses. He'd lay everything out on the table. His next wife would have no pretenses that he might actually grow to love her.

No, he wouldn't make the same mistake twice.

Dante headed immediately to the shower. But the water did little to smooth the rough edges of his rambling thoughts. Toweling off several minutes later, he accepted defeat. He wasn't going to be able to fall asleep anytime soon.

Though more than full, he grabbed a banana out of the fruit bowl on the small wooden table by the entryway. Just give his hands something to do.

Tossing it in the air and catching it again, Dante stepped outside and walked toward the patio, which was still lit up with lanterns. A movement to his right startled him as he sat down. Then he was staring into a small face with a pair of beady eyes, and short whiskers.

A monkey. And he was eyeing Dante's fruit.

"A bit clichéd, isn't it?" Dante asked the animal, who simply blinked at him and moved a dark paw in his direction. Dante could have sworn the little guy was actually pointing at the banana. A chuckle rumbled in his chest. Wait till he told Sierra about this tomorrow.

And there it was. He couldn't seem to get the woman out of his mind.

With a sigh, Dante leaned over and extended the fruit in the monkey's direction. He snatched it with amazing speed. Was it actually grinning at him now?

"Tsamaya kwa!" a deep voice ordered from the steps, and Banti appeared, shooing the monkey away with dramatic hand gestures. It responded with a series of low-pitched grunts before bounding away off the railing and into the dark, biting into the banana along the way.

Dante had to chuckle at the scene. His first real native fauna sighting and he hadn't even been on the game drive yet.

"I'm very sorry, Prince Dante. That vervet is a nuisance around here. This is much later than he's usually out. All the noise and commotion must have roused him."

Dante could relate. "I might have the same problem," he told the other man. "Speaking of which, you must be tired too."

Banti rubbed a palm over his face. "Yes, it has been a rather long day."

Dante gestured to the cushioned wicker chair next to him. "Have a seat."

Banti obliged with a weary sigh. "Thank you."

"Do you live here at the lodge?" Dante asked.

The other man shook his head. "No, I live in a village about six kilometers from here. I am usually home much earlier. But today was a special day. I was needed here at the lodge."

Dante felt a twinge of guilt. "Sorry to have been part of the reason that kept you from home. And from your family."

A wide smile spread over Banti's face at the last word. True affection flooded his features.

"Tell me about them," Dante prodded.

His grin grew wider. "I married the girl I fancied since I was a child. The smartest, prettiest girl in the village. So talented too. She weaves blankets that are true works of art. I'm so lucky she chose me."

Banti's love as he spoke of his spouse was so clear, it was nearly palpable. He was a lucky man, indeed. "Any children?"

He nodded. "A girl almost seven. Bosses me around like she's the parent." Laughter laced his voice as he spoke. "And a little boy. Just turned three." He reached in his back pocket. "Here, let me show you."

Pulling out his phone, Banti tapped the screen and scrolled a few times before extending the device toward Dante to show him a photo of a smiling woman holding a colorful blanket with a look of clear accomplishment across her face.

Banti scrolled once more to call up another photo. This one showed Banti with a small boy cradled in his arms and the same woman next to him, her hand resting on the shoulder of a little girl who stood between them both. The children had Banti's smile.

A picture-perfect family.

"You really are lucky as you said, my friend." Dante said the thought aloud this time.

The other man's grin suddenly faded. "I'm sorry. I should not go on like this. I know you lost your wife not long ago."

Dante nodded. "About two years now."

"I'm sorry," Banti repeated.

"No need to apologize," Dante reassured him, sorry that the conversation had turned to such a depressing one.

He never quite knew what to say when it came to his talking about his marriage, disastrous as it was. In more ways than one.

The lightheartedness of just a moment ago had vanished completely. Banti sat staring at him, his eyes warm with compassion. Mixed with a good portion of pity, no doubt. Dante was pitied the world over for having lost his spouse so soon after the marriage ceremony of the decade. A true debacle most of the world had watched. Rula had wrangled the publicity personally at great effort. Effort that had paid off. For a small island kingdom people barely thought about, their nuptials had been broadcast far and wide across the world. Exactly as Rula had wanted. He had indulged her, simply because he didn't care enough not to. Let her have the attention and limelight she wanted so badly. Dante had no doubt worldwide interest would fade quickly enough. And it had. Until the announcement that Rula was gone, having died tragically in a car accident in the Italian Alps.

"I recall it was an automobile accident, right?" Banti asked before Dante could come up with a way to change the subject. Apparently, he wanted to know more. Or maybe he thought he was doing Dante a favor by giving him a chance to talk about his lost wife. Given the other man's warm personality, Dante was guessing it was the latter. He did his best to find the words that seemed to satisfy the curiosity of those who asked.

"That's right," he answered. "She was on holiday to visit friends." The lie came so easily now after two years of telling it. Hell, he almost believed it himself.

The truth was much more sinister. Rula hadn't been in the Italian Alps to visit friends. She'd been there because she was leaving him.

He hadn't been able to love his wife enough to have her stay with him. And it had cost her everything.

But neither Banti, nor the rest of the world, needed to know that. So he continued to tell the lie. "She was out for a drive when she lost control of her car. There's speculation a falling boulder might have been the catalyst."

Banti blew out a low whistle. "My sympathies, man."

"Thank you," he replied.

Like countless times before when the topic came up, Dante would leave it at that. Of course, he couldn't divulge the whole story. The details that Sierra didn't even know. Details like the fact that his wife wasn't alone at the time of the accident. In fact, she'd been in the company of one of his most trusted advisers. The man had asked for an emergency leave the day before for "private reasons."

No, Dante wasn't going to share any of those details with Banti. It was a miracle that the press hadn't found out. Dante guessed it was enough of a story that the fantasy marriage of a royal couple had so tragically come to an abrupt end.

He supposed one day the truth might come out, but he'd worry about that when and if it ever happened.

"It must be difficult to carry out your royal duties without a partner."

"Thank you, Banti," he answered. Somehow the man sitting next to him now seemed more like a friend even though they'd met merely hours ago. "But I'm not quite ready to move on romantically. Not for a while."

"I understand. I'm sure your heart is still broken."

Dante ignored that. "Let's just say my wife would be a hard act to follow as the future queen of Nocera."

She must not have closed the netting over her bed all the way. Left a gap somewhere despite the miles of fabric draped over the canopy. Because there was definitely something in there with her, buzzing around and feasting on her skin. Sierra uttered a mild curse and kicked off the thin sheet covering with her feet. So much for getting some much-needed sleep.

Crawling out of bed to go look for some type of lotion, she heard the low rumblings of male voices outside. Apparently, she wasn't the only one still awake. Maybe there was someone out there who could help find some kind of balm for the itchy spots on her legs from the all the bug bites. Leaving her room, she made her way to the patio in the direction of the voices. Then nearly turned around when she noticed who it was out there and heard the last thing he'd said to his companion. Dante.

...*my wife would be a hard act to follow*...

Sierra started to pivot—she could deal with the itchiness until morning. Too late; he must have sensed her presence as he immediately stood. "Sierra? Is everything all right?" It took her a moment to answer, too distracted by the way his eyes roamed over her from head to toe. A silky tank and loose boy shorts that fell just below her thighs comprised her usual sleep attire. In this moment, she wished she was wearing something a tad less revealing. Why hadn't she thought to grab a robe?

"Yes," she finally answered. "I just seem to have a few bug bites. I was wondering if there might be some type of lotion available. To help with the itching."

Dante's gaze traveled over her once more. "Well, I can tell you your first problem."

"What would that be?"

He gestured toward her middle. "The color you're wearing. Tsetse flies are attracted to colorful clothing. That deep red is certainly colorful."

"I don't think what I'm wearing is much of the issue. Apparently, many beings find me fun to dine on."

A wolfish smirk appeared on his lips before he tightened them closed. Heaven help her, she'd noticed before he'd done so.

Banti broke through the tension that seemed to have thickened the air around them. "I have something you can use. I'll go get it. Though I have to warn you, it smells pretty bad."

She gave him a grateful nod. "Small price to pay. I'll come with you to get it."

No way she was going to stand out here alone with Dante a minute longer, his words from before echoing through her head. The image of the hungry expression on his face seared into her mind.

CHAPTER FIVE

SIERRA AWOKE THE next morning and scrunched her nose to the offensive stench that permeated the room. Banti hadn't been kidding about his remedy for the bites smelling bad. A complete understatement as far as she was concerned. Still, it had done the trick, allowing her to finally get some sleep. Restless as it was.

She'd been hounded by vivid dreams all night. Not quite nightmares but unsettling just the same. Images of her dancing around a large fire that grew and grew until the flames licked her legs. Her darting away from the heat only to fall into Dante's arms. He set her down immediately then reached for a golden crown that had materialized on her head before walking away, leaving her to evade the flames on her own.

Wow. A heck of a dream, one she didn't need a psychology degree to infer the symbolism behind.

Sierra shook her head briskly to push away

the images. Her imagination was in full active mode, which made sense; she was a creative professional after all. But at times like this it could be quite disruptive to her peace of mind.

Right. As if any part of this trip had been at all peaceful in any way. Today would probably be no different. Given that she and Dante would be attending their first game drive together. Of course, they would be in the company of the others, with Banti as their tour guide. Still. Why did everyone around them seem to be narrowing to a distance whenever she was in his company?

...my wife would be a hard act follow...

The sentiment wasn't surprising. The truth was, Rula was in a class all by herself. She always had been. Classically beautiful, and she'd always made sure to stay fit and trim. With a charming wit to boot. Of course, Dante wasn't going to get over her anytime soon. Sierra had never bothered to compare herself to the bright star that had been her dear friend. There wouldn't have been any point.

Sierra sighed and turned on the shower. There was no point in dwelling on any of this either. Once this trip was over, she could go back to her life in New York, try to make a real name for herself on the fashion scene. Everything would go back to normal. The fact that she'd already come up with new designs as a result of being here was icing on the cake.

She'd just shut off the shower and thrown on her clothes when a knock sounded on the door. Sierra glanced at the digital clock on the wall. Unless something about the plans had changed, she wasn't running late.

The person on the other side came as a surprise. The reporter. What was her name again? Cathryn? Caitlin? Katy? Something along those lines. "Yes? Can I help you?" Sierra asked, genuinely curious as to what this unexpected visit might be about.

Cathryn/Caitlin/Katy ducked her head before answering. "Sorry to bother you, but I wanted to catch you before breakfast. Do you have a minute to chat?"

Sierra immediately began to protest. "Any official statement—"

The other woman cut her off. "This is strictly off the record."

Sierra hesitated before opening the door wider to let the other woman in, out of curiosity more than anything else. She motioned for her to sit down at the settee in the center of the room, then took a seat on the wooden chair across from her.

"I don't mean to intrude, Ms. Compari." She actually looked nervous, further piquing Sierra's curiosity.

"Call me Sierra, please."

She smiled before saying, "Thanks. Please call me Cathryn."

That was one mystery solved. Now, to discover the reason for this visit.

"What is it that I can do for you, Cathryn?"

"Well, I'm a little embarrassed to even bring this up, but girl code."

Okay. That did nothing to clear up the reason she was here. "I'm sorry, girl code?"

The color rose in her cheeks, accented by her fair skin and reddish blond hair. Sierra was right, whatever Cathryn was here for, she was more than a little embarrassed by it.

"You know, I just want to be sure that I'm not stepping on another woman's toes. Or intruding on her territory."

What in the world was this woman talking about? Toes? Territory?

Then it snapped into place in her mind. Sierra felt her jaw drop as realization dawned. Dante. This visit was about Dante. Her suspicion was confirmed a moment later by the other woman's next question. "Is there anything—" she hesitated just a moment before pressing on "—anything romantic between you and the crown prince? Again, strictly off the record."

Sierra's mouth went dry as she tried to figure out a way to answer.

"I'm asking for personal reasons." Cathryn stated the obvious.

"I see," was the best Sierra could come up with in response.

Cathryn held her hands up. "I mean, I know it can't be anything serious. He is a royal, after all. But I wanted to make sure that you wouldn't be—"

Sierra didn't need further explanation. "A fling then?"

The other woman nodded slowly. "Can you imagine? An ordinary gal like me with an actual prince? That would make for a memory of a lifetime."

"I have no doubt."

"And before you say this isn't very professional of me, I just want to clarify that once I file this piece, I'll still have a few days here. On my personal time."

A storm of conflicting emotions rushed through Sierra. The most prominent one, she didn't even want to acknowledge—a stinging bite of jealousy. Pure and strong. Which made no sense. She had no claim to Dante. No right to feel even the slightest bit possessive. He was perfectly entitled to a fling with a journalist if he so desired. Consenting adults and all. So why was she finding it so impossible to just answer the simple question? Of course, she and Dante had nothing between them. Why in the world had this woman even speculated that she had to ask?

"But I wanted to make sure to ask you about it first."

Say something! Other than what she wanted to say most, that Dante held a special place in her heart that no one else had ever been able to fill. That she'd left her home kingdom and moved a world away rather than watch him make a life with the friend she considered a sister.

No, she couldn't say any of those things. She could barely admit it all to herself.

"No. There is nothing between the prince and myself. Feel free to make your move, Cathryn."

Just when Dante had decided Sierra was going to skip breakfast, she appeared in the doorway of the dining hall. A strange rush of pleasure almost overwhelmed him. But then he took a look at her face as her gaze found his. Something flickered behind her eyes, and she visibly bristled at the sight of him.

Huh.

Sierra clearly wasn't happy. And if he had to guess, he had something to do with that unhappiness. Which made no sense. He hadn't even seen her since last night when she'd hightailed after Banti to get her insect bite medicine.

"How's the itching?" he asked, standing as she approached the table.

"It's fine," she answered, brisk and short, before pulling a chair out and sitting down. At the very opposite of the table, as far from Dante as she could get.

A server immediately appeared with a steaming pot of coffee and a fresh cup for her. The smile she flashed the man was pure sunshine and warmth. Very different from the reception he'd gotten. Somehow, Dante figured it had less to do with caffeine and more to do with him. No, it was definitely him who had caused her ill humor, not some general state of irritation.

For the life of him, he had no clue what he might have done to cause it.

"You left so soon last night I didn't get a chance to introduce you to the new friend I'd just made."

"Friend?"

"Yep," he said, lowering his hand to knee level. "About this tall. Real hairy with beady eyes. Poor hygiene. I don't think he's showered in a while."

She blinked up at him. Clearly, his attempt at humor was falling flat. "A monkey," he explained. "Banti said he was a menace, but I found the little fella somewhat charming."

Her eyebrows drew together. If she was at all

curious about what he'd just said, Sierra was hiding it well. "Huh, you'll have to tell me all about him. Or her."

At another time was the silent yet implied addendum.

"Sure. Will do." Saints above. He'd had less trouble charming feuding dignitaries all those times he'd served as international mediator.

"Do you mind terribly if I have my breakfast alone?" She pulled a small booklet out of her pants pocket. "I wanted to work on some designs while I have my coffee."

Ouch. Far be it from him to stick around where he wasn't wanted. Still, he couldn't help the concern that grew in him that she would only be having coffee before the busy day they had in front of them. When was the last time he'd been concerned about whether a woman had eaten? He couldn't recall a single time, not even when he'd been a married man. Dante didn't want to examine too closely the ramifications of that.

"Sorry. I'll go and leave you to it. But I think you should eat something too. Coffee is hardly enough, given what we have ahead of us. Besides…" he added, gesturing to the extensive spread on the table—fruit, cheeses, various pastries and assorted breads.

She inhaled, her chest visibly rising and falling again dramatically. "Sure, I'll grab a bit while I draw."

Why did he get the distinct impression she was merely humoring him in her haste to have him disappear?

Without another word, Dante turned on his heel and made his way outside to the patio. Maybe his new friend the monkey would be more tolerant of his company. Even if Dante did have to bribe him with the banana he'd slipped into his back pocket at breakfast, just in case the vervet showed up again.

To think, he'd gone to the dining room early then lingered at the table, waiting for her to show up. Only to be effectively dismissed like some sort of pest. Like the tsetse flies that had been biting her all night.

That thought brought forth images of the way she'd looked last night. Her long shapely legs exposed under those, oh so short bottoms she'd had on. The way the tank had hugged her in all the right places and revealed the elegant slant of her shoulders.

Stop it.

The woman didn't even want to be in the same room with him right now, for heaven's sake. And he didn't even know why.

When he'd happened upon her drawing last night, she'd asked him to stay. So what had changed so quickly? Maybe he'd held her a bit too tight after catching her fall near the bonfire. Or he'd held on to her just a moment too long. Maybe he'd imagined that she'd been in no hurry to step out of his grasp. Or the way the glowing light of the fire had intensified the heat he could have sworn he saw in her eyes while she was in his arms.

He swore out loud. Enough already.

Well, Sierra could hardly avoid him all day. They were about to spend the next several hours together riding through the African grasslands. Maybe he'd manage to garner some clue as to exactly what he'd done to win her sharp ire. Judging by her pursed lips and rod straight spine, she wasn't going to divulge the reason herself. So different from what he was used to. When he was a married man, his missteps were pointed out to him almost immediately with great clarity by his parents or advisers as conduct unbecoming of a married prince.

Now, when it came to Sierra, he didn't have the slightest clue.

Sierra waited, watching through the doorway until Dante stood up and left the patio. Then she finally rose and walked out there herself, plopping herself down on one of the lounge chairs.

The sun was a dark, burnt orange, like an orb sent down from the heavens. It turned the clouds around it into a burst of color, various shades of red.

A large splashing noise sounded from the distance, coming from the direction of the meandering river. She wondered what kind of animal had just gone in for a swim or a refreshing drink. It triggered all sorts of pulse points in her imagination.

Opening up her notebook, she began to draw the idea for the dress that was slowly forming in her mind. She hadn't been lying to Dante when she'd said she wanted time to do some sketching. But she couldn't deny how petty she was being.

It made no sense. Why was she so annoyed with him? It wasn't his fault that another unattached female on this trip with them was interested in him. Sierra wanted to tell herself that she was merely perturbed out of loyalty to his wife. But she wouldn't lie to herself that way or dishonor Rula's memory in that manner.

The truth was as plain as the rocky hill in the distance. Her already complicated feelings for Dante were being pushed to the surface. And she didn't know what to do about it.

For heaven's sake. The man was a prince. The

heir to a crown. He was also a man who hadn't gotten over the loss of his wife and who had females yearning for him in the middle of southern Africa. What choice did she have but to keep her distance? For the sake of her sanity. And her heart.

Sierra sucked in a breath at the last thought. With a mild curse, she closed the book and crammed it back into her pocket. Though she had a clear idea of the dress in her mind's eye, suddenly her focus was too shot to try to draw it on paper.

A rustling in the trees in the distance had her wondering what kind of animal might be jumping through the branches. Maybe it was Dante's monkey. A chuckle spilled from her lips before she could help it. She really had wanted to hear about the encounter. But she'd been snippy to Dante instead. For something he wasn't even aware of. He had no idea one of the journalists accompanying them had her sights set on him.

How would Cathryn make her move? Sierra wondered. Would she show up at his door late at night? The woman was clearly not the shy type. Part of Sierra wished she could be the same. To just go after what she wanted, be bold enough to just announce it the way Cathryn had. The problem was, Sierra had no idea exactly what it was she wanted. Aside from her career, she had no idea what would fulfill or enrich her life.

One thing was certain—she had no social life to speak of. That would have to change. No doubt it was part of the reason her inappropriate and inconvenient attraction to Dante was making itself known. Sierra would have to find a way to fill that void. As soon as she got back to New York, she was going to take Camille up on the offer of the blind date with her cousin's friend. Or was it her friend's cousin?

It hardly mattered. Maybe Sierra would even sign up for one or more of those silly services that let you swipe left or right on your phone screen based on a simple photo and brief write-up. Sierra sighed and rubbed the tension out of her forehead. Rather than feeling any kind of excitement or anticipation at the prospect of a blind date or online dating, she felt pathetic and morose.

A shadow fell over her lap and she looked up to find Kaliha standing next to her chair. Sierra hadn't even heard her approach.

"Well, you look deeply pensive," Kaliha said. "How do they say…? A few lira for your thoughts?"

Sierra had to chuckle. "Not quite. Though I suppose it might work given inflation."

Kaliha narrowed her eyes on her in confusion.

"Never mind. I was just admiring the beauty of the skyline."

"Yes, lovely, isn't it?" Kaliha pulled the chair next to her and sat.

Sierra nodded. "Very different from the island nation I grew up on. Or the island city I call home now."

"Tell me about your birthplace. I mean your thoughts about it. Aside from what an outsider might know from simply reading an encyclopedia site." She patted Sierra's arm. "I've always wanted to visit but never got a chance."

For the first time that morning, Sierra felt a lightness in the vicinity of her heart. Thoughts of Nocera always lifted her spirits no matter her current state. "Oh, you must come see it. It's a mountainous island off the Greco-Turkish coast surrounded by the bluest, most tranquil waters that turn a shade of turquoise depending on the season. The beaches are as luxurious as any Club Med. Cruise ships from all over the world bring tourists to our pristine coast."

"And Prince Dante is the one who will inherit the throne of the monarchy," Kaliha said.

"Though I hope it won't be anytime soon. Long live his father, the noble king."

A pang of anxiety tightened in Sierra's center. How could she have forgotten for a moment the reason the king and queen weren't here themselves? The sole reason she was entrusted to accompany Dante on this trip was because the king's health was a concern. How selfish of her. She should be doing all she could to ensure the trip was a successful one. Instead, she was letting her schoolgirl crush impact her actions. The king and queen deserved better from her. And so did Dante.

She turned her focus back to the conversation at hand. "That's right. The monarchy of Nocera has always been a working family. Queen Naila supports various causes and charities throughout the world, such as the reason for this trip. And the king and Dante work hard to ensure the economy is healthy and robust, with a profitable export industry, everything from olives to citrus fruits."

Her mouth began to water thinking of the fruit trees she'd climbed when growing up. "The oranges and tangerines taste like nectar, especially picked straight from the tree. Which I did my share of when I was younger."

Kaliha gave her an indulgent smile. "Quite

the spokesperson. You might have a second career in the tourist industry. You sound like you miss it quite a bit, dear."

Kaliha was right. Sierra did miss Nocera and its people. More than she wanted to acknowledge.

CHAPTER SIX

BY THE TIME Sierra was dressed and had slathered herself in sunblock and bug repellent, she was running late. To her chagrin, everyone else had already gathered by the three-vehicle caravan that would take them on the day's adventure—a game drive through the nearby reserve.

Hurriedly, she made her way down the steps of the lobby toward the first open-air SUV. Dante stood leaning against it, his ankles crossed. Sierra's breath caught at the sight of him. The man looked like he could be posing for an African travel catalog. Or a cologne ad. Khaki pants belted at the waist and a fitted maroon shirt that showed off all the contours of his muscled chest. Dark aviator glasses with gold rims covered his eyes, so she couldn't quite read his expression as she approached. But the thin line of his lips told her he hadn't forgotten her coldness that morning. His words when he spoke confirmed it.

"You're set to be riding with me in the first car with Banti driving," he told her. "Unless you have an objection to that arrangement. If so, we can see about an adjustment."

She shook her head. "No objection. I'm anxious to get going. This is so very exciting"

With a small wave to the others behind them, she let Dante help her into the back seat then scooted over so that he could sit next to her.

Banti bid her a good morning and started the vehicle.

And then they were off.

Sierra did her best to focus on the landscape rather than the man sitting next to her. Luckily, it wasn't long before Banti was slowing down to show them something. When he came to a stop, he pointed to a tall patch of grass about three meters away.

"We're in luck," Banti said in a low voice. "Take a look."

Sierra didn't see it at first, but then a gasp of surprise and thrill escaped her lips. A spotted leopard lay resting in the blades of grass, licking at her paw.

"Oh, my. She's beautiful." Images flooded her mind with gowns of flowing fabric, covered in irregular spots.

"She's not alone," Banti added.

Again, it took a moment for her to see it. Squinting her eyes against the sunlight, she noticed a movement near the animal.

"Is that—"

Dante was the one who answered. "She's got a cub."

Sierra watched in awe as the small cat strolled around its mother, nuzzling against her with its button-sized snout. When it reached her backside, it swatted at its mom's swinging tail with its paw.

She turned to see Dante's reaction to the delightful scene to find another surprise. He was holding a professional looking camera to his face and snapping a photo. Sierra had been on enough photo shoots to know the equipment in his hands wasn't designed for amateurs.

Since when had he learned his way around a camera meant for a professional? He was handling it like he'd been doing it for years.

She gave him an inquisitive look when he lowered it. He merely shrugged. "Just something I picked up a couple of years ago."

A couple of years ago. That would mean right around the time of Rula's death. Even behind the glasses, she could see Dante was aware she'd figured out the timing of when he'd started his new hobby. A distraction from his grief then.

She didn't get a chance to ask any more about it as Dante leaned over, holding the camera out to her. "Here, look through the lens. To get a better look at the leopard and her cub. Better than the best binoculars."

He was right, Sierra realized as she did what he suggested. She felt as if she was standing less than a foot away. Instinctively, she reached her hand out, as if she could reach out and touch the leopard.

She heard Dante's low chuckle next to her. He was less than an inch away now, the camera still hung by a strap around his neck. The smell of his aftershave tickled her nose; the warmth of his skin brushing against her arms sent an electric current over her skin. For one insane moment, she imagined yanking the strap to pull Dante's face closer to hers. Then her lips would find his and she'd finally be able to taste him like she'd so often dreamed of doing. Her breath heaved in her chest at the pictures running through her mind.

Just. Stop. It.

Focus on the beautiful animal and its young one. Much safer than where her thoughts had just wandered.

She cleared her throat and handed the camera back to him. "Thank you. It was incredible to see her up close that way."

He shrugged. "You're welcome. Feel free anytime for the rest of the trip."

"Thanks," she repeated, unsure what else to say. She had no doubt she was going to take him up on the offer to look through his camera lens repeatedly through this adventure. Which would mean he'd be moving that close to her over and over. The scent of him filling her nostrils, his warm breath against her face. The way her body responded to his nearness. She had no choice but to try to ignore it all.

As best as she could anyway.

They lingered several more minutes simply staring at the scene in silence. Not a sound could be heard from inside the vehicle. It was if even their breathing had slowed as they took in the beauty of the scene. But an orchestra of noises played around them from the grasslands, like a concert performed by the wild. Insects and birds and running water. Along with a steady drumbeat that seemed to be ringing through the air.

Or maybe that was just the pounding of her heart.

He should have gotten a longer camera strap.

Dante shifted in his seat, moving away from Sierra and the sensations that rushed through him whenever she was close. The insect repellent lotion she wore couldn't mask her distinctive feminine scent. It reminded him of vanilla with a hint of cloves. She'd always smelled that way. Even dressed in safari friendly clothing, Sierra looked chic and fashionable, like the esteemed designer she was. A tan long-sleeved jacket over brown leggings that showed off the shapeliness of her legs. A loose scarf around her neck that matched the straw-colored cowboy hat she wore. She looked like some kind of novel cross between a female rancher and a fashionista.

He found it adorable. And more than a little enticing. Dante sighed. He should be noticing the sights around him instead of the woman in the seat beside him. Easier said than done.

Banti gave them a nod over his shoulder from the front seat then shifted the vehicle and they were moving once more. About three kilometers later, they approached another breathtaking scene. Clearly, Banti knew what he was doing as their guide.

To their right a few meters away on Dante's side stood four tall giraffes browsing and picking at the leaves of even taller trees.

"Those are acacia trees," Banti explained. "Giraffes are particularly fond of that type."

Without having to turn around, Dante sensed Sierra had moved closer to him to get a better look. He had to resist the urge to shift her onto

his lap so that they'd both be on the same side of
the vehicle. As tempting as that idea was, it was
out of the question, of course. So he did the next
best thing, he moved out of the way and handed
her the camera again, the strap tethering them
together once more. She held it up to her face
and her mouth fell open, forming a small o.

"They're majestic!" she exclaimed, breathless. "Absolutely beautiful."

The giraffes weren't the only things of beauty
out here. He cursed silently at the thought, then he
made a derisive sound and gave himself a mental
kick. Now he was waxing poetic like some sort
of besotted fool.

Sierra lowered the camera. "What?"

"Nothing. Just admiring the view." If she only
knew.

She gave him a speculative look before lifting
the camera back to her face. She held on to it
the entire time they were there, her chest heav-
ing with excitement at what she was witnessing.
One of the giraffes chose that moment to swivel
its long neck in their direction, as if watching
them the same way it was being watched. Sierra's gasp was audible.

She lowered the camera, eyes wide with awe.
"That felt like I was looking right into his eyes,"
she said, her voice shaky. Then she blinked and
looked down at the camera she held as if real-

izing for the first time what was in her hands. "I'm so sorry. I haven't even given you a chance to see." She held the camera out to him.

Dante immediately shook his head. There was no way he was going to diminish this experience for her by even a fraction.

"You hold on to it," he told her. "I can see just fine."

It wasn't until they'd driven away from the giraffes and Sierra handed the camera back to him that it occurred to Dante that he'd neglected to take their photo.

Their next sighting didn't take much longer to get to. Banti took a few wide turns, the terrain growing rougher with each one. Finally, they pulled up beside a formation of large boulders. It was Dante's turn to be awestruck. A pride of lions, including two with thick manes, lounged upon the rocks. As the Landcruiser came to a stop, the animals eyed them lazily, appearing rather bored.

Dante couldn't tear his gaze away. As stunning as the leopard and giraffes had been, the sight of a pride of lions was a different experience altogether. An element of danger hung palpable in the air. These animals were apex predators who might attack to kill on a mere whim. Knowing that they were in the capable hands of an experienced guide like Banti tempered the risk of course. Not to mention the two burly men in the last car serving as his bodyguards. But nothing could erase that risk entirely. Sierra's thoughts must have led in the same direction. She'd gone absolutely still next to him, her pallor the shade of a bleached bedsheet.

Without thinking, Dante reached over and took her hand in his, gave it a gentle reassuring squeeze. "They're not interested in us. Don't be afraid," he told her.

She visibly swallowed, her eyes never leaving the pride. "They're not interested now. But what if they suddenly get hungry?" she whispered in a low voice, almost imperceptible. As if she were afraid to disturb the lounging predators just a few feet away.

He had to chuckle at that. "That might be a problem."

"I'll say."

"Rest assured, I'll protect you at all costs," he said, with a dramatic clap of his hand to his chest. "Even if it means throwing myself in front of you in case of an attack."

She glanced sideways at him. "I know you're merely making a joke, but I fully expect you to do so if it comes to that."

He bowed to her. "Without question, my lady. I shall not even hesitate," he said, trying his best to sound like what he imagined a knight from medieval times might sound.

He extended the camera to her, but she held a hand up and shook her head. "No, thanks. I have no desire to see these guys up close. Not their sharp teeth or razor-like claws or…" She shuddered as she trailed off.

Dante began to get ready to snap a photo, not wanting to miss his chance when it came to this pic. But Sierra still held fast to his hand.

He didn't pull his hand away. It looked like he wasn't going to get a picture of the lions either.

Joking or not, Sierra's fear about the lions would have been tenfold higher if Dante hadn't been sitting by her side back there. Her pulse still hadn't returned to normal by the time they reached the clearing where they'd been having lunch middrive.

Though the rapid pulse might have had less to do with the predators and more to do with the man himself.

She watched Dante now as he helped Banti bring the coolers out while Sierra and the others set up the folding chairs around the makeshift table—a flattened bolder near a small stream. Dante had an easy way with almost everyone she'd ever seen him with. Now, he was chatting good-naturedly with the other man while he effortlessly lifted the handle of one cooler and carried it over to where she sat with the others.

Sierra felt ravenous. All the fresh air, sunshine and excitement of a game drive could sure work up a girl's appetite. Not to mention, the prospect of being the meal herself.

As soon as the sandwiches were delivered, she waited with no small amount of impatience until everyone had settled into their seats and unwrapped their portions. Then she tore into hers.

The crisp baguette and vegetable spread tasted better than any gourmet meal she'd been treated to at any five-star restaurant in Manhattan. The frosty bottle of water tasted better than the finest champagne. Or maybe she was just really thirsty.

She looked up to find Dante's gaze on her, amusement dancing in his eyes. Tilting her head, she gave him a small shrug. "I was hungry."

"Hope you saved some room," he told her.

"Why's that?"

He bumped her shoulder. "I eyed some chocolate chip cookies in one of the coolers. I think they're meant for later as a snack, but…" He reached behind him and pulled out a white paper bag.

Sierra glanced around at the others in the circle. No one seemed to be paying any attention to them. "You snuck cookies? How naughty of you. So unbecoming of a future monarch," she teased, keeping her voice to a whisper.

He shrugged, made a motion to put the bag back where he'd retrieved it. Sierra grabbed his upper arm to stop him. "Don't you dare put that cookie back."

Dante's smile thinned as his gaze dropped to where she touched him. His eyes darkened when he looked back up at her. A rush of heat swept through her, starting from the palm of her hand where she touched him. She dropped her hand back to her lap.

Sierra forced her mind back to the cookie. "I promise to share if you hand it over." He did so with a smile. Sierra polished hers off in a couple of bites. The others slowly scattered after their meals, strolling nearby, taking in the scenery.

Sierra simply felt too full and too hot to do the same. Whether Dante felt the same or simply stayed put to keep her company, she couldn't be sure. They were the only two left sitting at the "table," though Dante's bodyguards hovered nearby, somehow close enough to keep an eye on them while still affording them the ability to carry on a private conversation. She had to wonder what they thought about the two of them. Did they have the same suspicions Cathryn had about a potential relationship between them? The thought of the other woman and her interest in Dante sent a frisson of unwarranted anger down her spine. She didn't want to think about that right now. Or ever.

Sierra picked up a stick near her seat and started scribbling in the dirt by her feet. As comfortable as she was with the silence, she was curious about Dante's new hobby.

"So, how'd you come about getting a camera?"

His gaze turned to the horizon. "I needed a lot of time alone those first few days after…" He trailed off. Sierra didn't need him to finish the sentence. He was referring to Rula's accident.

"So many people offering condolences, pity really." He sighed wearily. "I'm ashamed to say that after a while I couldn't really stomach any more, though I know everyone meant well."

Sierra felt a pang of guilt. She could have been there for him, helped him in his grief. But she'd had to get away, had to find a way to deal with her own loss.

Dante continued, "Rather than hole up in my suite, I started taking long walks. First around the castle gardens. Eventually I wandered farther and farther out around the island. The beaches, the villages, wooded areas. Each spot had its own characteristic charm, its own beauty. And I'd never even bothered really seeing it before. It took a tragedy for me to even look at all the wonder I had around me since birth."

"You wanted a way to capture it permanently," she said.

He turned back to face her. "That's right. That's it exactly." He seemed surprised that she understood.

Sierra knew what he meant. "It's how I feel when I see something that calls forth an idea. What makes me want to sit down and sketch the images that come into my head as soon as they appear."

Something suddenly scurried by their feet, interrupting the conversation. A small animal that she wouldn't be able to name. It snatched a morsel of food someone had to have have dropped by one of the empty chairs, then ran back toward the tall grass with its haul.

"What in the world was that?" Sierra asked.

"Some type of Valhalian rodent, I would guess."

"It appeared to be the size of a small terrier."

Dante chuckled. "I guess rodents are bigger around these parts."

"Huh. I don't know. I think some of the rats in the New York subway system might be comparable. Particularly on garbage day."

Dante's eyes narrowed on her face. "What is

it?" she asked. Was there a smear of chocolate on her face from the cookie or something? If so, he might have mentioned it before all this time.

"Nothing. I just always wanted to ask if you're happy there. If you like it in New York."

Wow. The question came out of nowhere, wholly unexpected. The answer was complicated.

Dante continued, "After all, you're half a world away from your home and everything that's familiar to you. Is it all you hoped it would be?"

Huh. He'd clearly given this a lot of thought. How long had he been pondering such questions? What did it mean that he was still doing so?

"Maybe I simply wanted to see if I could make it on my own," she answered, though it was only part of the story.

He simply nodded. "I get that." He hesitated, as if he might be weighing his words, before adding, "Was that the only reason?"

Sierra sucked in a breath, waited several beats trying to find the words before giving up. "I had to leave, Dante," was all she said. "I couldn't stay there any longer." As far as answers went, she knew how inadequate that was.

But it was all she could offer him.

CHAPTER SEVEN

SHE JUST HAD to get through the next several hours. The event she'd been dreading this whole trip was set to begin in about four hours. Sure, Dante would be the center of attention, but she'd be front and center, and she had to be ready to answer any question directed her way. Not to mention all the photos. She'd watched Dante and his parents enough over the years to realize what a paparazzi magnet the royals could be. It was even worse when Rula was alive. Unlike Sierra, her friend reveled in the attention of the press, found ways to draw their attention and was always prepared to give them a money shot.

The activity in the lodge had grown considerably busier over the past twenty-four hours. The peace and quiet of the place when they'd first arrived was gone. Now, there were strangers with heavy equipment and large messenger bags traipsing around whenever Sierra stepped outside. Otto and the other bodyguard stayed much closer to her and Dante than they had been upon arrival. Both men seemed much less relaxed.

The entire atmosphere had changed.

Sierra sucked in a breath. She was just going to take the day one step at a time. Starting with the team that was on its way to her cabin to help her prepare for the news conference. The palace had arranged for a hair and makeup artist as well as an attire stylist. Sierra wasn't sure how she felt about that last professional the palace had insisted on. She was a fashion designer for Pete's sake. She clothed some of the most famous people on the planet and designed for the world-renowned House of Perth. But she wasn't about to argue with protocol. Sierra knew when to pick her battles.

Except you didn't fight for what you wanted when it mattered most.

Her wayward mind began replaying the days leading up to Dante and Rula's nuptials years ago. The moments she'd debated whether to let her true feelings be known. Or confided to one or both of them that they needed to rethink their marriage of convenience. Then common sense had intervened and she'd resisted the urge. How could she risk upsetting her closest friend right before she was about to marry a prince?

But maybe Rula would still be here if she'd done just that.

Her friend had deserved so much better. Rula's parents had only seen her as a means to an end—a way to ensure their elevation in Nocera's high society. On the surface, Rula appeared to have led a charmed life. Wealthy family, a beautiful home, close ties to the royals. But Sierra knew just how little love or true affection her friend had been afforded. And how much Rula longed for only that. Then when she'd finally married her prince, a tragic accident had claimed her life. Sierra's eyes began to sting with tears, and she fought to keep them at bay.

She pushed the errant thoughts away just as a knock sounded at her door. Throwing on her dressing gown, she ran to answer it. She'd been instructed to have her face scrubbed, her hair washed and be ready to get dressed. If only Camille was around to offer her some tips about being the one poked and prodded.

Two smiling faces greeted her when she opened the door. One carried a heavy silver case, the other was pulling a clothing rack. The woman with the case had an eyebrow piercing and a complicated bun of thin braids atop her hair. Her companion had deep ebony hair cut in a sharp-edged bob, slanted down from her ear to her chin on one side of her face, and an undershave on the other.

The woman with the pierced eyebrow introduced herself as Galen. The other woman's name was Tracey. Tracey was the stylist while Galen was there to do her hair and makeup.

"I'm a fan of your work, Sierra," Tracey said immediately upon entering the room, which made Sierra warm up to her instantly. Galen's warm, friendly smile was enough to do the same.

"Thanks." Sierra smoothed the skirt of her dressing gown. "I have to admit, I'm not used to being on the other side of this process. I'm a bit nervous."

"Nothing to be nervous about," Galen told her in a charming accent. She guided Sierra to her vanity bureau and pulled out the rolling chair in front of the mirror. Sierra sat down and studied her reflection. Dark circles framed her eyes; she hadn't gotten much sleep. Galen should probably start with covering that up first.

"Not just about all this," Sierra found herself admitting. "But about the news conference itself. I'm not used to being in the spotlight."

Tracey walked over and gave her a reassuring pat on her forearm. "I'm sure you'll do great. And with our help, you'll look absolutely stunning up there."

Her looks weren't her only concern. Not even in the top three, in fact. She was much more worried about saying the wrong thing, making a fool of herself by appearing unknowledgeable. Demonstrating that she didn't belong up there with the likes of Crown Prince Dante Angilera.

Behind her, Galen bent down to lean over her shoulder. "You are going to have to try to relax," she said with sympathy. "I can't apply color to your lips when they're thinned out like that. And the foundation will cake on your forehead if you don't stop creasing it."

That was the second time she'd been told that in the span of a few weeks. Hadn't Camille mentioned something similar back in New York? She really had to work on it apparently.

"I'll do my best," she promised.

Tracey pulled out her cell phone. "I think we're going to need some kind of guarantee. Something to soothe your nerves." She made a call and spoke low into the phone. Within moments, a server appeared at the cabin door with a rolling cart of chilled sparkling wine and ripe fresh fruit.

"Now, just remember how knowledgeable you are and how successful you've been. You can do this," Galen reassured her, combing out her hair while Tracey poured wine into three long-stemmed glasses.

"That's right," Tracey added. "You're going to knock their socks off. I have no doubt."

By the time the two women were done with

her, Sierra felt less like she'd been prepping for a major news conference and more like she'd just attended a fun girls' night out. Galen's and Tracey's cheery attitudes and encouraging words had taken some of the edge off her nerves and helped to alleviate some of the sadness the memories of Rula had brought forth earlier.

She'd barely touched her glass of sparkling wine, yet she was much more at ease about facing all those journalists and cameras.

Not that she was looking forward to it in any way.

Dante had to remind himself to breathe when he saw Sierra approaching the makeshift stage where he, Sierra and a group of conservationists would be taking questions. Some kind of transformation had taken place since he'd seen her last. He knew the palace had arranged for some kind of stylists to help her prepare. But he didn't pay much attention to such things.

He was certainly paying attention now.

Her hair was done up in some kind of tight bun at the base of her neck. The navy dress she wore fell just below her knees and showed off her tanned lower legs. She was carrying a tablet and a stylus pen.

She looked like a cross between a serious solicitor and the sexiest, most alluring cover model. A potent combination that had his libido jumping to life.

So not the time.

They were here to face a slew of press to answer questions about the reason for this trip and about Maman's foundation. He had to focus.

By the time he assisted Sierra to the chair next to him and the questions began, his breathing had just started to return to normal. Somehow, he managed to get his brain to work enough to deliver the response for any question directed at him.

To her credit, Sierra was holding her own despite her being a novice when it came to such events. She jumped in at various moments to make relevant points and even cracked a joke at one point that had the entire group chuckling.

When it was all over, Dante finally let himself breathe a sigh of relief. The news conference could undoubtedly be called a success. A lot of that success could be attributed directly to Sierra. She'd performed like a star. He shouldn't be surprised, but the woman seemed to be able to impress him at every turn.

He had no doubt that she was completely unaware of just how impressive she was.

The next morning seemed to go past in the blink of an eye. With the news conference over and the press gaggle working on filing their interview stories, some of the pressure of royal duty had begun to taper. Nothing official was scheduled on the itinerary. Only an activity Kaliha had spontaneously arranged for them to celebrate a successful Q and A with the reporters—a river cruise. Dante spent the hours until then going over the photos he'd taken on the game drive and organizing them in a file on his tablet.

Funny enough, he had just as many pictures of Sierra on his camera's memory card as he did the sights and animals they'd seen. He hadn't even realized he'd taken so many of her. Sierra staring at an exotic bird as they drove by an acacia tree. Sierra adjusting her hat to wipe away a loose tendril of hair. Sierra smiling at the sight of a large flock of quelea birds flying overhead in the sky.

In the photos he'd taken on the game drive, she looked carefree and casual, enjoying herself. Her sun-kissed cheeks and bright smile adding to her already photogenic features. Yesterday, she'd looked regal and composed. The transformation had been rather striking. Either way, she was breathtakingly beautiful. Something he was certain she wasn't aware of. Sierra Compari could give the runway models she worked with a run for their money.

But there was more to her. So much more.

The way she'd deftly answered the questions thrown at her by an overzealous gaggle had sent a surge of pride and admiration through him. Sierra had been ready with facts and data, better prepared than he could have hoped for. Maman knew what she was doing when she chose her as his companion on this trip.

Dante paused in the act of cropping a photo. He was dangerously approaching Sierra Compari fanboy status, and he had to get a grip already.

He would have to show these pics to her. But then he would have to explain why his lens had found her as the subject so often. Damned if he'd be able to come up with a plausible explanation. He should have at least included one or two of the prime minister and his wife who'd been traveling in the other car. He would have to be sure to do so today aboard the cruise.

The cruise. He glanced at his watch. It was just about to time to meet the others and ride to the Chobe River, where they would board a luxury houseboat and stay overnight drifting on the water.

Kaliha had arranged it for them after the game drive to give them a taste of the more luxurious excursions Valhali had to offer visitors and tourists. Something told Dante the woman was ready for a bit of luxury herself.

Saving the files and powering down the devices, he grabbed his overnight bag and made his way to the meeting spot in front of the lobby. Banti was already there, scrolling through his phone. He greeted Dante with his usual wide smile when he saw him approach. The prime minister arrived with his wife a few moments later.

Finally, Sierra appeared. In her typical fashion, she arrived at the agreed upon time right on the dot. Never later, not even a moment sooner. Pretty efficient, he would have to say. He was about to ask her how she managed to do so for every single meeting, but then he got a look at her as she came down the steps. Words escaped him. If he thought she looked beautiful yesterday, today she looked downright jaw-dropping.

The jade green wrap dress she wore draped her curves in all the right places and fell just above her knees to expose shapely calves. The color brought out the specks of gold in her hazel eyes. She had her hair up in a clip, showing off her neck and the delicate gold earrings dangling from her lobes. Fabric sneakers a shade lighter than her dress rounded out the ensemble.

She held a different hat from the one she'd had on the other day. This one much was more decorative, with a ribbon wrapped dangling over the brim.

Stunning was the first word that came to mind. Followed by a litany of others that he would never dare say out loud.

Banti took her bag and loaded it in the back of the SUV with the others. She flashed everyone a wide smile. "Good afternoon."

Kaliha and Nantu responded in kind. Dante still couldn't find his voice, so he simply nodded. He hadn't seen her at breakfast, figured she'd taken it in her room. It had been worth the wait.

Resisting the urge to stare during the drive, he tried to focus on the scenery instead. Lucky for him, the two women kept up a constant flow of chatter during the ride. By the time they reached the river twenty minutes later, he'd finally managed to eradicate the wholly inappropriate images flooding his mind and starring Sierra. Images of her unwrapping that dress from her body and having it fall to the floor. Then he would… A tingle ran down his arm to his fingertips.

Stop it.

There he went again.

"Something wrong?" she asked him, her eyebrows furrowed. He hadn't realized he'd actually said the words out loud. How embarrassing. He had to get a grip. The sight of a woman in a dress had turned him into a mound of putty and it was completely unacceptable.

"Just anxious to board," he said. "Looking forward to this cruise."

"To take more pictures?"

"Something like that."

She pointed at his chest. "Where's your camera?"

He motioned to the car with his thumb. "Packed away safely in one of the bags back there."

"Same as my sketchbook," she said with a smile that had his gut tightening. "I'm certain this outing is going to trigger a slew of inspiration." Excitement resonated in her voice.

"I can't wait to see what you'll come up with," he told her, absolutely meaning it. Surprising, really. He'd never been interested in women's fashion before.

When they reached the bank of the river, a tender boat about eight feet long awaited to take them to the houseboat in the middle of the river. Nantu helped his wife to board and Dante reached for Sierra's hand to do the same before Banti could reach her.

Banti noticed and gave Dante the slightest smirk but didn't say anything. Though he shot Dante more than a few knowing looks as they approached the larger vessel and boarded.

Smiling members of the crew greeted them

on the deck. One held moist towels while another handed them frosty glasses of ruby red punch.

Then they were off. Sierra walked to the railing of the boat, her smile growing wider as her gaze darted from the water to the woodlands in the distance. She appeared to be trying to decide which part of the landscape to focus on.

Whereas Dante knew exactly where he wanted to look.

She would have to thank Kaliha for setting up this trip.

As much fun as the game drive had been, this was a different experience altogether. Sierra felt like she'd just checked into the Waldorf, the houseboat was that ritzy. Only, the hotel was floating on one of the most breathtaking rivers in the world. She'd seen pictures of the Chobe on various travel sights before upon learning she'd be traveling to Valhali, but none of them had done the river justice.

The water was a shade of azure blue she'd never seen, the riverbank dotted with all sorts of fowl. Thick cotton ball clouds hung in a baby blue sky with the sun shining bright.

Her senses were in complete exhilaration mode.

Whatever lucky star had led her to be here

today, she was more than grateful. Dante strode over to stand next to her. She had him to thank as well. Dante was the real reason she was here.

He pointed to the distance. "You see that?"

She followed the direction of his finger, her mouth falling open upon realizing what he was pointing to. "Is that a crocodile?"

He nodded. "It sure is," he said, then added, "Wait. Maybe it's an alligator. I never could keep track of the difference."

She laughed at his exaggerated confusion. "Either way, it's a sight to behold. I've never seen one of those outside of a zoo."

"Don't you want to get your camera," she asked, "to take pictures of all of this?"

He shook his head slowly, turned his focus on her face. "I think I'll just enjoy the scene firsthand today rather than through a lens." His gaze never left her face as he answered her. The words were innocuous enough, but the tone in his voice and the way he was looking at her with darkened eyes sent a shiver of awareness down Sierra's spine.

She couldn't help where her mind drifted, imagining how things might have been between them if circumstances were somehow different. If fate had given Sierra a far different role in the life of Nocera's crown prince.

The idea that she might be enjoying this out-

ing with the man she loved was almost tear in-
ducing. If Dante were her man, he might step
behind her now, wrap his arm around her waist
as they took in the view together. He might nuzzle her neck then turn her face toward his, tilt
her chin to drop a soft kiss on her lips. A soft
kiss that might lead to longer, deeper ones.

She looked at him now. He hadn't bothered
to shave, and a hint of a beard dusted his chin.
The wind ruffled his hair. What would it feel
like to run her hands through the waves at his
crown? Or to feel the stubble on his chin against
her skin. A shudder racked her body.

"Where did your thoughts just drift off to?"
he asked, his voice velvet rich. Heaven help her,
he sounded as if he knew the answer to that
question, and that possibility had her insides
shaking.

My wife would be a hard act to follow.

His words from the other night drifted
through her head. How could she forget for even
one moment what the true reality actually was?
There was no way Dante could ever be more
to her given their history. Rula's death had left
a gap his life that Sierra could never fill. He
would be monarch one day. The woman Dante
needed by his side at that time had to be someone more befitting the role of queen. A woman
who could hobnob with the upper crust. Some-

one who knew how to entertain heads of state or movie stars and felt at home among people like that.

Just like Rula had been.

"Sierra?" Dante asked, pulling her away from her meandering thoughts. That's right. He'd asked her a question, hadn't he? But it wasn't as if she could answer it truthfully. So she changed the subject. Leaning at the waist over the railing, she gestured downriver. "Look. Water buffalo."

A herd of the animals stood huddled together on the riverbank, muzzles in the water for a refreshing drink. Others simply lay on their stomachs, to seek relief from the heat.

"They're not as big as I would have thought," Dante said. A conflicting swirl of emotions ran rampant in the pit of her stomach. Relief that he'd allowed her to dodge his question. But a twinge of disappointment as well. She felt further conflicted when Banti walked over to stand by them, shutting the door fully on the intense moment between her and Dante. For now.

"Come to the other side," he told them. "You're in for a treat."

Sierra and Dante followed him around the cabin to the other side. Banti hadn't been kidding. A large herd of elephants splashed in the river, their trunks spouting water like fire hoses. They ranged in size from a small house to small calves. The little ones dropped and rolled, splashing each other and their parents.

"It's absolute chaos," Sierra said, delighted laughter bubbling free.

Her laughter faded as she noticed one of the older calves hovering off to the side. When it did move, it was clearly hobbling. "What's wrong with that one?" she asked Banti. "Is it hurt?"

"I see what you mean," Banti said, then stepped to the cabin and came back with a pair of binoculars. When he lowered them from his face, his eyes were dark with worry.

"It's hurt," he said. "There's a large gash on one of its hind legs."

"What might have caused it?" Dante asked.

Banti shrugged. "Several possibilities. It might have been attacked by another elephant. It does happen in certain circumstances. Gotten too close to a snare. Or a predator took a swipe before momma and the rest of the herd chased it away."

"Oh, no. Poor little guy." Sierra's eyes stung, feeling for the poor animal who had to be hurting. "What will happen to it?"

"Don't worry. I'll arrange to have a veterinary team come out first thing to search for the herd and to treat the injured calf. The team has an excellent tracker, and the lead vet listens to me."

"Are you two close friends?"

He shook his head. "There are times I want to launch him into the desert," Banti answered, with zero edge in his voice, but more of a tone laced with what might be described as affection. "But, yes, we're close. He's my younger brother."

Sierra breathed a sigh of relief. In her concern over the calf, she hadn't even noticed until now; Dante had taken her hand in his own. He gave it a comforting squeeze.

He had to admit the truth to himself. He didn't want this cruise to end. He didn't want this trip to end. Because once this was all over, he would have to go back to reality. A reality in which everyone wanted something from him. Where nothing but responsibility and duty awaited him from sunrise to sunset.

Who was he kidding? He'd never been one to shirk the demands on him. What he didn't want to end was time spent with Sierra. He'd always been fond of her. Both as a friend and... well, more. But this trip had awakened that part of him that he'd pushed aside for as long as he could remember. That part of him that had called to Sierra instead of the woman he'd been duty bound to marry.

Dante waited for the familiar flood of guilt to wash over him at such thoughts. Guilt that was always there, simmering just under the surface. To his surprise, the wave was just ever so slightly weaker than usual.

Now, as he waited above deck while Sierra freshened up for dinner, he wasn't sure how well he'd be able to continue hiding the truth. That he had feelings for her. Even though he knew how wrong it was. How disruptive to her life it would be to ask for anything from her.

Not to mention his own. As it was, Maman pestered him daily about this princess or that heiress she wanted him to meet. Each one of them bringing their own contribution to Nocera in the form of a trade agreement or much-needed import.

It was always about Nocera.

He sensed Sierra's approach before he saw her. The now familiar tightening in his gut every time she was near alerting him to her presence. His breath caught in his throat when he turned to face her.

She'd removed the clip from her hair, which now fell in soft waves around her face and down her shoulders. The fabric sneakers had been replaced by strappy leather sandals that revealed brightly colored toenails.

Saints above. He was noticing her toenails.

Clearing his throat, he held his arm out to her. "Ready to go to the upper deck?"

She nodded with enthusiasm. "More than ready. Something smells delicious."

He led her up the steps to the higher level, where several highly polished wooden tables had been set up with place settings and tall, lit candles.

Pulling out her chair at the nearest table, he sat down opposite her. They had a clear view of the river below and the setting sun in the sky above. A gentle breeze rustled the trees in the distance.

"Are we the first ones to arrive for dinner?" Sierra asked the server who appeared immediately once they'd sat down.

The young woman filled their glasses with water from a frosty pitcher. Several wedges of lemon floated on the surface above the ice. "It will be just the two of you, my lady," she answered when she was done.

Huh. That was rather unexpected.

Sierra's eyes grew wide. "Just us."

The woman nodded. "The prime minister sends his apologies. He wanted you to know that he's suffering from a touch of motion sickness, so he and his wife will be dining in their cabin."

"What about Banti?" Dante asked. He'd given his bodyguards permission to stay in their cabins if they so pleased; it wasn't as if he needed protection aboard a boat traveling down a river. Both men had apparently taken him up on the offer.

"Banti is good friends with our captain. They are eating belowdeck to catch up."

Right. The prime minister's queasiness was one thing, but why did Dante get the impression that Banti's absence was due to an ulterior motive? Recalling the knowing smirk the man had had on his face during the drive to the river, Dante had his suspicions. He wasn't sure whether he wanted to thank the other man or ask what in the world he'd been thinking.

Sierra rubbed her hand over her chin, then started fidgeting with her earring. He might say she was nervous.

"Don't worry, Sisi. I won't bite." He knew better but couldn't seem to resist teasing her.

Her eyebrows lifted clear to her hairline. "I'm not worried, Dante. Just hungry."

Right.

"And concerned about Nantu," she added a moment later.

Again, not terribly convincing.

She went on, "Plus I wanted to ask Banti whether he'd gotten word to his brother about the wounded calf."

That all was undoubtedly true, but her assurances were clearly a case of "doth protest too much."

Was she really that nervous to be alone with him? The way she ran her finger over the rim of her water glass gave him a small clue as to the answer.

Curious. What had her acting so anxious about dining alone with him? He had to admit, it was a rather romantic setting. Aboard a triple-decker boat floating gently on the Chobe River, the sun setting in the sky casting a luminous glow on the surrounding clouds, the sounds of wildlife echoing through the air. Anyone witnessing the scene might think they were a couple in love on vacation or even on their honeymoon.

"We haven't seen any hippos yet," she said, completely changing the topic at hand, snapping him out of fantasyland. In a rather clever way, actually.

"I'm sure it's just a matter of time," he said.

She nodded. "I hope so. I'll keep on the lookout while we eat."

The server appeared with salads and a steaming basket of bread rolls, followed by another server carrying a large platter of barbecued meats.

Dante watched as Sierra dug into her food, her

eyes darting from her plate to the landscape then back. She wasn't making eye contact with him.

He would have to find a way to change that, put her at ease so that she could begin to enjoy the evening as much as he was.

Once again, it occurred to him just how badly he didn't want any of this to end.

The universe was toying with her. There could be no other explanation. How else would one explain the way she found herself dining alone with Dante aboard a romantic cruise in one of the most stunning settings on earth? Particularly after the way she'd reacted to him earlier that afternoon when they'd first boarded.

She absolutely could not be falling for this man. He was the last person on earth she should be lusting after.

Lust. That's all it was. It wasn't as if she was falling in love or anything. Sierra stopped short, her fork raised halfway to her mouth. Except that she was. There was no way to deny it any longer. If it were at all possible, if the circumstances were different and life was fairer, she'd give herself over to this man. Completely.

The thought could easily send her spiraling into a panic attack.

Just a few more days. Once this trip was over,

she'd go back to her own life, try to forget that any of this had even happened.

Only, these weren't the kind of memories a woman might easily forget. Another thing that scared her.

The truth was, she'd be thinking of this time spent in Africa for the rest of her days. She would compare every man she met to Dante, and without a doubt they would all come up woefully short. He was charming, handsome, witty. Everything a warm-blooded woman with a pulse might want. Even without the whole prince angle.

As for him, she had to wonder what his return to Nocera would be like. Would he feel any kind of nostalgia for the time they'd spent together? She thought of the way he'd looked at her on the lower deck earlier, the huskiness in voice as he'd spoken. Would he recall any of it?

Probably not. Most likely, he'd simply return to his princely duties, resume honoring the memory of his deceased wife, and eventually find a replacement who ticked off all the appropriate boxes.

Sierra barely tasted her food before it was cleared away. A shame, really, it was so well prepared, the meat tender, the bread crusty on the outside and soft as cotton candy inside. The side vegetables were crisp and fresh. But her taste buds weren't quite registering. Her mind was too scattered, her heart too full with feelings she'd tried to keep at bay for too long.

So when dessert arrived accompanied by a tall cocktail with a sugared rim, she took the glass without hesitation. Liquid courage and all. She downed it much faster than she should have, ignoring the dense chocolate mini cake on her dessert plate. When the server appeared with a replacement glass, she didn't refuse.

"Sierra?" Dante's rough voice reached her from across the table.

She kept her eyes leveled on the drink in front of her. "Yes?"

"Weren't you supposed to be the lookout?" he asked.

What on earth was he talking about? "What?"

He gestured toward the water. "You're missing the hippos."

She snapped her head up, then zoomed in on the riverbank. He was right. Not one but two gray leather-skinned hippos swam leisurely in the water. A small bird was catching a ride on the back of one of them.

"Wow, they're magnificent. Though I hear they can be vicious."

"They can be ferocious, as can any wild animal I suppose," Dante said. "Though hippos are known to be particularly aggressive and dangerous, not only because of their large size but also because they have very sharp teeth."

He flashed her a grin followed by a playful wink. "I can give Banti a run for his money."

Sierra returned his smile. "Hey, if the whole prince thing doesn't work out, you can start a second career as a tour guide out here."

It was a ludicrous statement. Dante Angilera was the crown prince of Nocera, a role he was literally born into, and would perform with utmost grace and success. Which reminded her of all the reasons she had to keep her feelings toward him in check.

Suddenly, the excitement at seeing the hippos and the headiness from the liquor evaporated into thin air. Dante clearly sensed the shift in her mood. "Something the matter?" he asked, concern etching lines at the corners of his eyes.

Sierra wiped her mouth with the cloth napkin. "I'm suddenly very tired," she lied. "Probably all the food."

He tilted his head, studying her. "Or perhaps the two days of nonstop adventuring."

"That too," she said, rising out of her chair. "I think I'll retire. Now that the hippos on my check list can be crossed off."

Dante stood. "I'll walk you to your cabin."

"That's not necessary, Dante. Please stay and

enjoy your evening." But her protests were futile. He'd already reached her side.

"I insist," he told her.

In silence, they made their way to the bottom deck, which housed the suite of guest rooms. Finally, they reached her door.

"I guess I'll see you in the morning," she told him, reaching for the doorknob.

But he made no move to leave. Against her better judgment, Sierra lifted her face to look at his, immediately realizing what a mistake that was. She should have twisted the doorknob and stepped into her cabin without another word or hesitation. The way Dante was looking at her had her knees weakening. A dipping sensation settled in her midsection that had nothing to do with motion sickness.

Dante's eyes landed on her lips, hooded and dark with emotion. Without knowing she intended it, she stepped closer to where he stood, their mouths now barely an inch apart. That tempting scent of his aftershave teased her, had her mouth going dry.

"Sierra." Her name on his lips sent a shudder through her core.

"Yes?"

He blinked, swallowed. "Good night. Sweet dreams." Then he leaned toward her. The next instant somehow his lips were on hers. Time stopped. As did her heart beating in her chest.

Sierra couldn't help the moan that escaped her as Dante's mouth fitted over hers. He cupped her chin with one hand, the other resting at the small of her back. Every point of contact sent a burning warmth over her skin. She ran her palms up his arms and over his shoulders, relishing in the feel of him against her. Nothing could have prepared her for the longing and desire coursing through her body. Finally, Dante was in her arms, kissing her with abandon, and she was certain she'd never be able to get enough of it. Enough of him.

He tasted like citrus and mint and some exotic spice she wouldn't be able to name.

He tasted as good as she'd always known he would.

A peck on the cheek. That was all he'd intended. But something had gone awry. One of them had turned the wrong way, at the exact instant they shouldn't have. He couldn't even be sure which of them it had been. But the next moment, his mouth was on Sierra's. Her soft delicate lips like rose petals against his own. She tasted that way too. As sweet as the smell of fresh roses in the spring. Or the finest honey or nectar.

He meant to pull away, he really did. But then

the soft sound of her moaning under his lips sent a surge of burning desire over every cell in his body. And he was lost.

Fate played a hand when the boat hit some kind of wave and jostled her further against him. Or maybe he'd pulled her closer himself without even thinking. The sail had been smooth up until now, after all. She was pressed against his length, running her hands up to his shoulders.

Heaven help him, he wanted to ask her to invite him into her room.

But that would have to be her offer to make. So he stopped himself from asking her outright. For now he would enjoy the moment, enjoy the feel of her, the taste of her.

It would be over all too soon.

He couldn't get the kiss out of his mind. Dante tossed and turned in the darkness of his cabin, sleep eluding him now for hours.

Nor could he erase the image of Sierra's face when they'd finally broken apart. Stunned, wide-eyed. Like a startled doe. Then she'd turned and darted into her room without a word. He'd shocked her. Well, he'd shocked himself. And maybe it was merely his masculine pride, but he'd felt her pleasure as clearly as he'd experienced his own. For one thing, she hadn't pulled away immediately. Her mouth had lingered on his. Exploring, prolonging the moment. He wanted to kick himself for not prolonging it any further while he had the chance. Because he wouldn't get another one in this lifetime.

He'd have to come up with something to say to her; they couldn't exactly ignore that the kiss had happened. The only question was, what exactly was he supposed to say? That he was sorry? That would be a lie. He hadn't intended to kiss her. But he didn't regret that it had happened.

He wanted to do it again.

Which was sadly out of the question, of course. He could explain away one time. As a momentary loss of judgment. A friendly peck that had somehow turned into something else, which was true enough.

The pretending that he didn't want to do it again would be a lie. But only out of necessity, because he had no choice. He couldn't very well have a fling with his dead wife's best friend. The thought of the kind of worldwide gossip that would create had him cringing where he lay. Dante could just imagine the juicy headlines plastered all over the websites or magazines. There were journalists back at the lodge they'd be returning to, for Pete's sake.

Not that any other kind of romantic relationship with Sierra was an option either. She had a life back in New York, had made no secret of the fact that she didn't consider Nocera her home any longer. It would be the only home Dante would ever know given his birthright.

No, any kind of real relationship with Sierra was impossible. As was any kind of fling.

Which left him in quite a predicament, didn't it? Because the taste of her still stubbornly clung to his lips. And he wanted more of that taste than he had a right to.

CHAPTER EIGHT

UNLIKE THEIR DINNER last night, Sierra hadn't found herself alone with Dante since they'd left the houseboat and returned to the lodge.

A heavy awkwardness hung between them now, their conversations stilted and stony. She knew the others had noticed, if the speculative glances cast between Kaliha and her husband were any indication.

They couldn't spend the rest of the trip that way.

Determined to prove to him that their kiss on the cruise was nothing to be skittish about, Sierra made her way to his room. They could be adults about this. The kiss had happened. It wouldn't happen again. That was that. Yet she had no idea how she was going to go about saying any of that. She'd figure it out once she got there.

She was only a few feet away when Dante's door opened. But he wasn't the one who stepped out over the threshold. Sierra's steps faltered, and she nearly tripped over her own feet.

Cathryn.

Ha! So much for the reporter's declaration that she would wait until she filed her story before she made her move. Apparently the temptation had been too much.

It looked like Sierra didn't need to see him about their misbegotten kiss at all. He'd clearly already forgotten about it, while she'd been reliving the kiss in her head ever since she'd felt his lips on hers.

Sierra pivoted on her heel to head back to her own room before the other woman could lay sight on her. She had no interest in discussing the way Cathryn and Dante had spent the afternoon together. She could just imagine how that might have been.

Not that it was any of her business. Cathryn had been blunt about what she was after when it came to Dante. And Dante was a grown adult who'd been single for quite some time. If he wanted a meaningless fling while on a safari, it was his prerogative and his own business.

It had nothing to do with her.

So why were Sierra's fists clenched so tight that her fingernails were digging into her palm? Taking a deep breath, she loosened her fingers, sprinted to the door to her cabin, opened it then shut it firmly behind her. Then she started pacing the wooden floor.

Sierra let out a bitter laugh. She was such a fool. Served her right for making more out of a silly kiss than it had obviously been. Dante had simply been lost in the moment. A romantic dinner on a luxurious cruise must have that effect sometimes. He'd probably gone back to his room last night and slept soundly, without giving Sierra or their solitary dinner another thought.

A cry of horror escaped her lips as a realization occurred to her. That could have been so much worse. What if she'd made it to Dante's door and knocked on it only to find Cathryn in there with him? He would have seen the shock of humiliation on her face right away. He knew her well enough.

See, she should consider herself lucky. Someone up there was looking out for her. Saving her from herself. So why did she feel like smashing something against the wall?

Or collapsing in a crying heap?

Sierra spent the evening in her cabin, asking for a tray of sandwiches and fruit to be delivered to her instead. The right call. The solitude had done her a world of good. She'd even managed to get some sleep.

Maybe it was cowardly of her, but the risk of running into Dante, or worse, into Cathryn with Dante, wasn't one she'd been ready to take last night.

But she couldn't stay holed up in here another minute longer. For one thing, she wanted to find Banti and ask if his brother had been able to check on the wounded elephant calf yet. On top of everything else, she hadn't been able to stop thinking about the poor little guy and wonder how he was faring. Silly, really. There had to be hundreds of wounded or hunted animals out there right at that very moment. But she hadn't seen any of those others firsthand. Hadn't watched one of them hobble in pain as it had tried to keep up with the others only to fall over.

The calf had tugged at her heartstrings, and she hurried her shower then toweled off in record time to go see where Banti might be. There was nothing on the itinerary today as Nantu had a daylong conference call about another problematic poaching incident outside the village. Banti's brother must have his work cut out for him. Being a vet out here had to be demanding and draining.

Sierra wandered the grounds until she found Banti behind the workers' quarters hosing off the Landcruiser. He put down the hose when he saw her.

"Good morning, Sierra. I missed you last night at dinner."

She wondered if Dante had been at dinner. And if he'd been alone. Sierra had to stop herself from asking the question out loud. "Thanks, Banti. I just needed some downtime."

He cast a smile at her. "Fair enough. Are you feeling rested then?"

"Sure am. I wanted to ask you about the calf. From yesterday. The little one who was hurt."

Banti's eyes softened. "You have a good heart, don't you?"

Sierra wasn't sure how to answer that, felt mildly embarrassed at the question. Did she? Sometimes she felt selfish and self-absorbed. How many decisions had she made in life out of a desire to protect herself from any hurt?

"Did your brother and his team get a chance to check on him?" she asked, refocusing on the matter at hand.

He glanced at the large watch on his wrist. "They should be doing so right about now. Or at least trying to. Mama elephants can be very protective. I was going head out that way. See how it went and say hello to my brother."

"Is there any chance I can tag along? If it's not a nuisance, that is. I'd love to be able to witness how they take care of a wounded calf."

"No nuisance at all. Though we'll have to

keep our distance. Can't get in the way of the veterinary team."

Sierra tapped two fingertips to her forehead. "Got it."

"Give me a chance to dry off the car and we can be on our way." He grabbed the thick towel thrown over his shoulder.

Sierra noticed another one folded on a stool nearby and took it in hand. "Only if I can help."

Within moments, the thirsty towels had the Landcruiser clean and dry. Sierra climbed into the front seat next to Banti and they drove around the quarters toward the lodge.

They didn't get past the patio. Dante jumped the three steps and reached the vehicle in a flash of movement that could only be described as agile and athletic.

The smile he flashed her sent a shiver down her spine. Stupid. Stupid. Stupid. The man had probably spent the night in the arms of Cathryn the reporter.

"And where are you two sneaking off to?"

Banti put the vehicle in park. "No sneaking. I was going to go see my brother and his team take care of the wounded elephant calf. Sierra wanted to come along."

Dante turned his gaze on her. She resisted the urge to look away and meet his eyes straight on instead. "You've been worried about the little thing, haven't you?" he asked her. Rhetorically apparently as he didn't wait for an answer. "I'm not surprised, knowing you."

What was she supposed to say to that? Thank you?

He didn't give her a chance to decide, turned his attention back to Banti. "Mind if I come along too?"

Sierra sucked in a breath. No. No. No.

That was the last thing Sierra wanted or needed. Aside from her concern about the baby elephant, she was hoping for a few hours without the risk of running into Dante. But she could hardly be the one to answer. Her heart sank as she knew what the man's answer would be. There was no reason to turn Dante away. Not for Banti anyhow. Sierra herself had all sorts of reasons.

"What about your bodyguards?" she asked.

Dante shrugged. "They're not with me twenty-four seven," he answered. "I'll be back before they'll notice I'm gone."

"Then, sure," Banti said, restarting the ignition. "Hop on."

Bingo. She'd been right. Great. Just great. Rather than avoiding him, now they'd be spending the next few hours together. So much for that great entity above who she'd thought was looking out for her yesterday. Apparently, she had decided to take the day off. Dante jumped into the back seat before the last word was out of Banti's mouth.

"You don't mind if I'm along for the adventure, do you, Sierra?"

Another rhetorical question clearly. And a belated one. What could she possibly do about it now, after all? Ask Banti to stop the car and send him back to the lodge? How in the world might she explain why?

"It's not for me to say how you spend your time, Dante," she answered over the roar of the engine.

How true a statement it was.

If the cold shoulder Sierra was giving him from the front seat was any frostier, it might send the searing heat lower several degrees. What was it about the woman? She seemed to run hot and cold without any kind of warning. Today it was the latter.

The kiss. That had to be why her hackles were up. Was he to apologize for it then? The notion didn't sit well with him. Still, it was clear they needed to talk about it at some point.

One more thing was clear—Sierra didn't want him along on this little jaunt. Well, too late now. He was already here, and he wasn't about to turn back. They drove most of the way in silence, save for Banti occasionally pointing out an exotic bird in a branch above or spots that might have been dens for wild dogs. At one point he stopped the car so that they could listen to the call of a roaring lion. Soon they rounded a bend and another SUV came into view. A van was parked beside it.

Several meters from the vehicles stood the herd of elephants. Four men were nearby. One of them appeared to be trying to lure a small calf toward him with what looked to be a large watermelon, while keeping an eye out for the calf's mother. Another man in green fatigues stood nearby with a lasso. Dante figured they were trying to isolate the injured calf.

Banti parked the vehicle a prudent distance from the veterinary team. "This is probably as close as we should get," he said over his shoulder.

They sat in silence for several moments. The rushing sound of the river providing a soothing backdrop to the scene unfolding before them, a crystal blue sky overhead. Dante reclined in his seat, admiring the men trying to help the wounded animal.

The peaceful atmosphere didn't last long. In the next moment, all hell seemed to break loose. It happened so quickly, Dante thought he might have been imagining it. A large elephant seemed to explode out of the nearby river. Before any of the men could do anything, the elephant charged at the man who'd been approaching the calf. Presumably, that man being Banti's brother.

He'd guessed right. Banti shot out of the vehicle and ran toward the chaotic scene. "Stay here you two," he yelled behind him.

Sierra jumped out of her seat, her hand to her heart. She'd gone pale, her eyes wide with disbelief.

Dante reached her side, took her tightly in his arms. She was shaking. "Hey, it's all right. The elephant seems to have stopped its attack."

Which appeared to be the truth. The animal was standing in one spot, pounding its foot into the ground with menace. But it wasn't charging. It was over before it really began. But the damage was done. The vet sat squirming on the ground in pain. Banti and the other men lifted him gently and carried him back to the van.

Banti ran back a few moments later. "I need to get you to back to the lodge."

Dante held a hand up to stop him. "How is your brother?"

Banti sucked in a breath, his hands trembling at his sides. "We don't know for sure yet. The good news is the mother elephant clearly only meant to scare him. She was protecting her calf."

"Good, that's good," Sierra said in a breathless whisper. She didn't sound terribly convinced anything was good at all.

Banti continued, "But Tiejo needs to be checked out. We need to make sure there's no serious damage." He jumped into the front seat and started the Landcruiser. "I'll get you two back to the lodge then I'm going to head to the clinic to check on him."

Dante gripped the man by the shoulder. "Banti, go. Run back there before the second car leaves. I'll contact someone at the lodge to bring us back. I'm sure they'll be here in no time. Go be with your brother."

Banti hesitated, his eyes darting from Dante to where Sierra stood, clearly torn. "I don't know…"

Sierra stepped over to where he stood, touched his forearm. "We'll be fine. Go, Banti."

Banti hesitated just another moment before bolting back toward the other men, yelling at them to wait. They heard him just in time.

Dante waited several beats until his breathing returned to normal. He'd felt so helpless just now, unsure of what to do. But the best course of action seemed to be to get out of the way.

Sierra had been mesmerized by the chaotic

incident, shocked, but some of the color was beginning to return to her cheeks. He reached into the back trunk to the cooler where he knew Banti kept the water bottles and handed her one.

"Thanks," she said, opening the lid and taking a long drink. Her shaking had slowed considerably as well.

"You're welcome," he answered, then held out his hand. "Mind if I use your cell phone?"

She blinked at him. "Cell phone?"

"Yeah, you know. So we can call someone at the lodge and tell them to come get us."

Sierra blinked some more, and he had a sinking feeling in the pit of his stomach. Then she said the words he was dreading. "I didn't bring my cell phone."

Not good. Because his was sitting back in his room at the lodge.

"Don't tell me," Sierra said, her voice shaking. "You don't have yours either."

"How do I answer if you don't want me to tell you?"

She swore, using such an unexpected, uncharacteristic term that Dante couldn't help but laugh, despite their dire circumstances.

"What part of this is funny at all?" she demanded to know.

"Relax. I'm sure there's some kind of communication device in these vehicles." But when he reached for what looked like a receiver and pressed the various buttons, all he got in response was a bunch of loud static.

Sierra leaned over his shoulder. "Do you mean to tell me we're stranded out here? With no way to contact the lodge?"

Dante shook his head at her. Did she really have such little faith in him? "Relax, Sierra. The SUV is equipped with GPS. I'll just use it to figure out how to get back."

Her shoulders sagged with relief, and she blew out a deep breath. "All right, please try not to get us lost."

"Oh, ye of little faith," he said, putting the vehicle in gear and turning it around in the direction in which they'd come. The GPS monitor was different from anything he'd seen before, but he was betting he could figure it out through trial and error as they drove.

And that's when it started to pour.

Yep, her so-called protective spirit was definitely MIA. Either that or a vengeful deity was toying with her, one who'd just opened the skies to pour buckets of hard, punishing rain over her and Dante. Only one of them deserved it, she thought with no small amount of pettiness. For the record, that would be him.

For his part, Dante looked absolutely miserable. The expression of shock and dismay he currently wore would be funny if their current situation wasn't all so…well, unfunny.

Within seconds, she was soaked. Her clothing plastered to her skin. Her hair a soppy mess atop her head. Water was starting to pool in the floor of the vehicle.

"Now what?" she asked over the noise.

"Hang on," Dante answered, navigating the dirt road that was quickly turning to mud. "I have an idea." Then he mumbled a few words under his breath that sounded something like "if I can figure out how to get there."

The "there" turned out to be a large sprawling tree. At first, Sierra figured Dante meant to park underneath the branches as cover from the rain. But when she realized where they were, she had to begrudgingly admit that his idea was even better than that. Looking up, Sierra saw there was a good-sized tree house nestled among the branches. Shelter!

As angry as she was with him, at the moment, she wanted to fling her arms around his neck and smack a big, wet kiss against his mouth.

Steady.

"I noticed it when Banti was driving us down," he told her, shouting over the sound of the rain. "Let's get up there."

Sierra ran to the base of the tree, where a

spiral series of steps began about a foot off the ground. She was about a third of the way up when her soggy shoe slipped and she dropped three steps. The good news was a set of strong hands stopped her fall before she dropped any farther. The bad news was that she'd practically landed on Dante behind her, and he was now cupping her rear end to keep her steady.

"Whoa, are you okay?" he asked, his mouth against her cheek, his breath hot on her skin.

As fine as she could hope to be with his large palms wrapped around her backside.

"Just great," she answered, then resumed her climb. Moments later, they were both stepping through the doorway into the tree house. The rain pounded heavy on the roof, but it seemed to be holding strong.

"What is this place for?" she asked, stepping all the way inside. The house was the size of her closet back home. Tight quarters, but at least it was a dry roof over their heads.

"I'm guessing it's some sort of lookout for hunters," he answered, wiping the moisture from his face. He'd let his facial hair grow even longer. His wet hair curled around his tanned face. He looked like some kind of rugged rancher or misplaced cowboy. And wasn't this a swell time to be noticing such a thing? But even now, in his soaked clothing and with his dark hair plastered against his forehead, Sierra couldn't deny the man was simply drop dead handsome. She could hardly blame Cathryn for making a move on him. Heaven knew, if their circumstances weren't what they were, she would have done the same. Sierra might have been the one leaving his room yesterday having spent a pleasurable afternoon in his arms, in his bed.

A shudder racked her body.

Dante breached the short distance between them. "You're cold."

He began rubbing her upper arms in an effort to warm her up. Little did he know, the effect of his hands on her only served to amplify the cause of her shudder. She stepped out his grasp with no small amount of reluctance. What she wanted to do was step deeper into his embrace. Wrap her arms around his neck and lose herself until she could forget where they were and how they'd gotten into such a precarious predicament.

"Thanks. I think I'm good now," she said instead.

"You sure? You're still kind of shaking like you're cold."

She would go ahead and let him believe that mistaken assumption. Better than having him guess what had really caused her body's reaction at being so close to him.

"Wait here," he told her. "I'll be right back." He stepped back out through the door.

Wait? He'd really told her to wait? As if there were any choice in the matter. What else would she do? Where did he think she might possibly go?

When he reappeared moments later, he was carrying a large duffel bag. One she'd seen in the back of the Landcruiser when she'd been helping Banti towel it off earlier.

"There might be something useful in here," he told her, dropping the bag by her feet. "I also threw in some snacks out of the cooler. In case we're here longer than we want to be."

That was already the case as far as she was concerned. She was tired, cold and wet. So very wet.

Just for something to do, she unzipped the bag and opened it. "For a pampered prince, you're pretty resourceful in an emergency."

He had to know she was teasing him. Dante had completed Nocera's required military service and had been deployed in some of the most dangerous places in the world on humanitarian missions. He was far from pampered.

"Thanks? I think," he said, crouching next to her to look through the bag.

To Sierra's relief, the bag appeared to contain emergency supplies for just such an occasion, including a towel. Thin and small, but a towel none the same. There was also a fleece blanket in there, along with a flashlight, some wipes and a long canvas tunic of some sort. Like the towel, it was rather thin. But it was dry.

"Thank God. This stuff will come in handy." She yanked out the towel first.

"Great," he agreed. "That's good. Now all we have to do is wait out the storm."

"Right. We can try to dry off in the meantime."

How long could it rain, anyway?

Dante couldn't recall a single time he'd been in a tree house before. He didn't exactly come from the type of family that went camping or built forts in trees. However, there was a first for everything.

"What's that?" Sierra asked behind him.

He hadn't realized he'd spoken the last few words out loud.

"Nothing," he told her, then glanced out the square opening in the wall. "Just wondering if the rain is tapering down at all."

"I don't think it is. Unfortunately."

Sierra stood toweling herself off with the square of a towel they'd found in the duffel. She might as well have been raking the ocean. Water dripped from her hair, her clothing, even her nose.

He thought she looked adorable. But she was clearly uncomfortable. Dante reached inside the bag for the tunic he'd seen in there then held it out to her. "Why don't you put this on? You'll feel better once you're wearing dry clothes."

She eyed it with speculation. "What about you? You're wet too."

He shrugged. Being soaked didn't really bother him. Despite Sierra's shivers, he didn't find it cold at all. Especially now that they'd found shelter from the wind. "It's not really my color." Not to mention, the thing wouldn't even reach his knees.

She took the tunic out of his hands, did a twirl motion with her finger. Dante turned his back to her.

"I hope Banti's brother is all right," she said behind him.

He hoped so too, but it was hard to concentrate at the moment. All he could think about was the fact that Sierra was undressing merely a foot or so away. He heard the sound of a heavy thud as she dropped her wet clothing to the floor. Which meant...well, it was obvious what it meant.

Focus on something else. Anything else.

It wasn't easy, but Dante forced his attention

on his surroundings instead. The rain pounded heavily on the wooden roof, but the underside stayed dry. All in all, the place was pretty well constructed, not so much as an uneven floorboard.

A red-breasted bird with black wings and head landed on the sill of the window. Dante began to turn around to ask if Sierra was seeing it. He caught himself just in time. He didn't really need to defend himself against any Peeping Tom suspicions right now.

After what seemed like an eternity, Sierra finally finished changing. "I'm done," she said. "You can turn around."

Dante wasn't sure what he'd been expecting. But the sight of her had him struggling to keep from reaching for her and pulling her into his arms. Somehow, she made the simple tunic look incredibly sexy. It draped over her curves like the finest designer dress, reaching just below her knees. Not exactly see-through but thin enough that his mouth had gone dry, and he had to avoid looking in the vicinity of her chest.

Yeah, he had it bad.

She spread her arms wide and did a slow 360-degree turn. "You know, it's pretty plain and a little drab. But with the right accessories, I think I can make it work."

She had no idea just how well the tunic was

working for her already. "If anyone can pull it off, it's you."

She glanced around the small room. "You'd think these hunters might have furnished this place. You know, in case a couple of clueless stranded tourists needed to wait out a storm in here or something."

"Yeah, well, wild game hunters aren't exactly known for their consideration or hospitality."

He didn't want to tell her about his real suspicion about this place. His best guess was that it was used by poachers to track their game.

Sierra crossed her arms in front of her chest. "So, now I guess we just wait."

"Not much else to do until the rain clears up."

"I guess not."

"May as well make ourselves comfortable," Dante said, grabbing the blanket and scrunching it up on the ground by the wall. "Your seat, my lady."

Sierra sighed, lowered herself to the floor and sat on one end of the spread blanket. Dante hadn't forgotten the feel of that luscious bottom in his hands when she'd lost her footing climbing the tree earlier. And he wouldn't forget it anytime soon.

Sierra tucked her legs under her and patted the stretch of blanket next to her. "There's room for both of us," she said, then added, almost under her breath, "Though it will be tight." She didn't sound thrilled about the prospect.

Dante sat down, making sure to avoid any contact. He was still dripping wet whereas Sierra at least had managed to get dry.

"I can't believe neither of us have our cell phones," Sierra said with a shake of her head. "I didn't think to grab it because I thought I was just going to ask Banti about the elephant calf then head right back to my room."

Dante nodded once. "Makes sense."

"What's your excuse?" Sierra asked.

He shrugged. "I didn't think I'd be leaving the lodge either. And my phone needed to be charged. I was on it most of last night speaking with my father."

"Long conversation?"

"He was catching me up on all the developments back home, so that I can hit the ground running as soon as I return."

"How is he?" Sierra asked. "Your father?"

Dante leaned his head against the wall. So many ways to answer that question. "Still being monitored by his team of doctors. No real change." But there was no denying that Papa was getting older. Each year, his energy level dipped a little lower, his health giving them another small scare. Dante would have to pick up more and more of the king's responsibilities and eventually take over altogether.

He had to be ready.

Dante rubbed a hand over his face. Plus at some point, probably fairly soon, he would be expected to remarry. Nocera's people would be waiting on Dante to provide heirs of his own. They needed reassurance, stability in their leadership.

So much to think about before it all came looking for him.

Was it so wrong to try to forget about it all while he was a world away with Sierra by his side? Reality would intrude soon enough. Despite the disaster this day had turned into, Dante knew the demands on him wouldn't make life any easier when he did get back home.

Judging by the pounding rain on the roof and the messy view out the window, the storm wasn't abating even a little. Sierra adjusted the neckline of the tunic and shifted in her "seat." Dante immediately moved over to give her more room. As if another inch was going to make a difference. As it was, the close quarters were wreaking havoc on her senses.

"Bet you're sorry now that you asked to come along with Banti and me this afternoon."

He nudged her shoulder with his. "And miss all this alone time with you?"

"The last time we were alone, we were on the houseboat." Why in the world had she brought that up? For all she knew, Dante might have forgotten all about that night. Forgotten about the way he'd kissed her outside her door. He certainly wasn't acting like he remembered any of it, not their isolated dinner. And certainly not what had happened afterward. He'd even had a liaison with Cathryn since then.

His tongue darted out to lick his bottom lip. "Yes. I recall."

He could have fooled her. "Huh. Surprised to hear that. I was beginning to doubt that it happened at all." She hadn't meant to say that, almost an admission, like she was some sort of jilted lovesick teen with a crush who'd ignored her in the high school hallway. How pathetic of her.

Dante sighed deep, his chest falling. "Look, Sierra," he began. "I know it was inappropriate of me, what happened on the houseboat."

Really? That's where he thought she was going with this?

He continued, "I lost myself for a moment."

"I see," was all she could come up with to say.

"It won't happen again."

Ouch. Sierra felt a tightening in her midsection, not quite sure what to attribute it to. He was right, of course. But as the cliché went, it took two to tango. They were equally to blame. She shouldn't have kissed him back. She should have stepped away instead, bid him a polite goodbye and locked herself behind her door. But sharing the blame didn't take the sting out of hearing Dante say he regretted it had happened, that he wanted to take it back.

At least she had some answers now.

"You sound awfully close to apologizing, Dante," she said, faking a lightness in her voice that she didn't feel. "There's hardly any need for that. I got carried away too. It was just a meaningless kiss. Let's just agree to leave it alone."

He nodded slowly, his eyes roaming over her face. "Sure thing. If that's what you want."

"It is," she lied.

That settled it then, didn't it? Their little interlude on the river last night was all sorted. Dante had simply been carried away with the romantic setting. He hadn't meant to kiss her. She didn't need to give it another think. Good thing. Because she suddenly felt so very tired and weary. In both body and mind. Leaning her head back against the hard wooden wall, she slowly let her eyes close, then focused on the darkness behind her lids. The pattering of the rain outside served as a meditative background soundtrack, almost. She just needed a moment to breathe, a moment of silence.

When she opened her eyes again, the world around her had changed. It took a few seconds for Sierra to get her bearings, but two things registered immediately. For one, the rain appeared to have stopped; the humming background noise of the storm was gone. All she heard now were the myriad of jungle noises that had become so familiar these past few days. For another, she could see through the square opening in the wall that served as a window that the sun was shining once more.

Okay. Clearly, she'd had her eyes closed for longer than she'd thought. In fact, she must have fallen asleep.

There was more.

Something else was different about her surroundings. Something much more alarming. Sierra was no longer on a flimsy blanket on the hard floor. Apparently she'd shifted in her sleep to find a more comfortable accommodation. On Dante's lap!

His arms were wrapped around her, cradling her against his chest. Her head was tucked under his chin. The scent of him filled her senses. For a moment, she was too stunned to move. Finally, she made herself blink away the remaining grogginess of sleep and try to pull herself together. She had to remove herself from Dante's grip before he awoke.

Too late. Before she could so much as move, he blinked his eyes open. Heat immediately darkened their depths. His arms around her tightened ever so slightly. Sierra's heart pounded in her chest as she tried to come up with something to say, words that might cut the tension or somehow lighten the mood. But her mind had gone blank. Dante blew out a deep breath. His hand reached up from her waist to cup her face. Sierra forgot how to breathe. Several moments passed in loaded silence. Both seemed to have forgotten how to speak.

Finally, Dante's lips parted. "Hey, Sisi." He spoke the nickname softly, his breath hot on her lips. "I gotta be honest about something."

"Yes?"

"I don't think I'm going to be able to keep my earlier promise."

Her mouth went dry, her tongue felt heavy. "You're not?"

He shook his head, oh, so slowly. "No. I'm afraid I'm going to kiss you again, after all."

Heat rushed through Sierra as she braced herself. She wasn't going to stop what was about to happen, though she knew well that she should be doing exactly that. But she didn't want to.

Dante tilted his head closer, lifted her chin with one finger.

Sierra's body seemed to move of its own accord. Her hips rotated just enough that she was squarely on Dante's lap. The intimate contact had her breath hitching in her throat. Still, she couldn't seem to make herself move away so much as an inch. Dante's clothes were still damp, seeping moisture through the thin fabric of her dress straight through to her skin. The heat darkening his eyes told her he felt every sensation she was feeling. Sierra leaned closer, inching her face toward his.

The loud noise of static sounded from below. Another noisy burst followed a second later.

Dante blinked twice. Then he gave a brisk shake of his head.

"What is that?" Sierra asked.

"It's coming from the Landcruiser outside," Dante answered, his voice rough, and heavy with desire. "I think it's the radio."

It took several moments for Sierra to process the words. Her body was throbbing at every point it connected with Dante's. Her mind a scrambled mess of desire and confusion. Then she finally managed to come to her senses, and she suppressed a horrified sob. She was ready to give herself completely to this man, atop a tree house of all places. Scrambling off his lap, she leaped to her feet.

Dante rose slowly, his gaze never leaving her face. "Guess we better go answer that," he said.

She couldn't find her voice to respond, so she merely nodded then followed him down the tree's steps to the car.

CHAPTER NINE

HEAVEN HELP HIM, he'd almost done it again. What in the world was wrong with him? Dante returned the receiver to the dashboard after listening to Banti's instructions about how to work the GPS and get them back to the lodge. It was a wonder he even processed the man's instructions. His insides were still a churning mess. Waking up with a beautiful woman on your lap, one you'd been attracted to since as long as you could remember, would do that to a man.

Dante righted the wheel of the vehicle after hitting a rather large dip in the muddy terrain. He had to slow down. They'd turned down Banti's offer to come get them as the tree house was halfway to the lodge as it was. But he was already anxious to get back there to rip off these wet clothes then take a long hot shower. He glanced over at Sierra in the passenger seat. She still wore the tunic but had also wrapped the blanket around herself. No doubt she was looking forward to showering as well.

Too bad they couldn't do it together.

When they arrived back at the lodge a few minutes later, Banti awaited them by the patio. He gave them a once-over and lifted an eyebrow in question. "Are you two all right?"

Dante nodded, stretching his legs. They still felt tight and stiff from the hour or so spent sitting on a hard floor with Sierra on his lap. Not that he was complaining about that last part. It wasn't likely that would happen again anytime soon. "Just need to get cleaned up. And then maybe some food. Speaking of which, you're going to need to restock the supplies in your emergency kit."

"Sorry about leaving you. That freak storm wasn't on any radar. If I'd known, I would have never—"

Sierra cut him off, wrapping the blanket tighter around herself. "Banti, don't apologize. We're fine. How is your brother?" she asked.

Banti clasped his hands together. "He's going to be okay. Just a few scrapes and bruises. Like we thought, the calf's mother was only trying to protect her baby. Tiejo treats the ailments and vaccinates the herds that regularly stop at that point in the river. She must have recognized him on some level so as not to cause any real damage."

Sierra's shoulders dropped a couple inches in relief. "Thank goodness."

Banti continued, "And the team went back to treat the calf. He was isolated from his mother and given the necessary vaccines to aid his recovery."

"Good news on all fronts, then," Sierra said. "Now, if you'll excuse me. I could really use a shower and need to find some real clothes."

Too bad, Dante thought, watching her walk up the steps then head toward her room. She did look rather fetching in her current state. He'd been telling the truth earlier; Sierra really did pull off the disheveled look rather well. Then again, she was the kind of woman who would look good wearing a potato sack.

"You sure you're all right?" Banti asked again. "You look a little dazed."

He *felt* a lot dazed. Desire still coursed through his body, the need to chase after Sierra and pull her back into his arms almost overwhelming. "I'm fine," Dante answered, clapping the other man's shoulder in reassurance. Except for the bruising his ego had taken earlier, that was.

Sierra's words sounded in his head again. *It was just a meaningless kiss. I got carried away too.*

"If you say so," Banti said, looking unconvinced. "You just seem kind of out of it."

A rather apt description. His mind was still trying to process what had happened.

She'd told him just minutes before that their kiss on the houseboat hadn't meant anything to her. Had he been imagining it then? Her reaction? She'd appeared angry with him for the past couple of days. The kiss had to be why. He couldn't think of any other reason for it. So he'd felt the need to explain himself and his behavior the previous night.

"Dante?" Banti's question pulled him out of his thoughts. Oh, yeah, he'd asked Dante a question.

"All good, my friend. I just didn't get much sleep last night on top of all the chaos of the afternoon." That was all true enough. He was spent, between the hours-long phone call with the king and being stranded in a storm, it was no wonder he'd almost made the mistake of kissing Sierra again back at the tree house.

He really had to get a better hold of himself.

"I'll go have the kitchen prepare you two some sandwiches then."

"Thanks, Banti. And I'm glad to hear your brother is okay." He was no wildlife expert. But it wasn't hard to imagine the damage a large elephant could do to a man if it wanted to.

"Thanks. Those sandwiches will be ready in no time. Should I have them sent to your rooms?"

Dante shook his head. "I can't speak for Sierra. But I think I'd prefer to eat out here on the patio once I get changed, to enjoy the poststorm fresh air." First, he would have to get the lecture from Otto over with. The bodyguard was not going to be happy with him. Dante had left the lodge for hours without even a cell phone or so much as a heads-up to the other man.

"You got it," Banti answered, and turned to head toward the kitchen. "I don't blame you. There's nothing like the aftermath of an African rainstorm."

Dante wasn't going to admit the truth out loud. The fresh air excuse was just that, an excuse. He wanted to come back out here in the hopes that Sierra would make her way back outside too.

It made no sense really. Despite being up close and personal in tight quarters just now, damned if he couldn't wait to see her again.

Sierra took so long under the steaming spray of water, her fingers and toes were pruned by the time she turned the shower off.

A message pinged on her cell phone. She

reached for it where it rested on the end table, vowing to never leave the room without it again.

Heat rose to her cheeks when she thought about the way she'd moved onto Dante's lap in her sleep. Not to mention her reaction to him upon awakening.

If it wasn't for Banti's call on the vehicle's radio, she shuddered to think of what she might have done in her groggy, disoriented state. She had to thank her lucky stars that static from the radio had sounded when it had.

Take that, vengeful deity! Banti had been her guardian angel in this case, coming to her rescue in the nick of time before she made a fool of herself again. She must have still been waking up and had been dreaming the part where Dante said he wanted to kiss her again. No way that had really happened. After all, he'd practically apologized for doing so the first time.

What was it about the man that had her forgetting herself so easily?

The message on her phone had been sent by the man in question. Dante wanted her to know that a tardy lunch had been prepared just for the two of them and awaited her on the patio.

Clipping her wet hair in a topknot, Sierra threw on a pair of jeans, a long-sleeved cotton flare blouse and slipped on a pair of hiking boots. Her stomach rumbled in anticipation. The granola bars from the duffel bag weren't much in the way of sustenance.

When she stepped outside, the effects of the unexpected storm still lingered in the air. Tendrils of steam still rose off the wet ground in ghostlike curls. The heels of her boots sunk into gooey mud as she made her way to the patio.

Dante sat in one of the lounge chairs, and a silver tray sat before him on the wicker center table. Next to it was a steaming teapot. Her stomach rumbled again, and the thought of a soothing cup of tea almost had grateful tears swimming in her eyes.

Dante stood when he saw her. He hadn't touched any of the food yet. Sierra couldn't help but feel touched that he'd waited for her.

"You clean up pretty well," he told her with a small smile. "Not that you didn't look great in a tunic with a blanket cape."

He really had to stop saying such things to her. Sierra knew it was all in jest, some lighthearted banter. But the words made her feel a certain way nonetheless. A way she had no business feeling. As it was, look at what her imagination was doing already when it came to Dante.

"You didn't have to wait." She lowered herself into the seat opposite him. "I'm sure you're as hungry as I am."

He'd changed into a pair of khaki pants and a teal-colored V-neck shirt that emphasized the tanned color of his skin. Both to her delight and her dismay, she noticed he still hadn't shaved the stubble from his face.

"What kind of gentleman would I be if I ate before the lady was present?" he asked with a playful wink. There he went again.

She ignored his question, took one of the cucumber sandwiches off the tray. Dante poured her a cup of tea without bothering to ask. Not that he needed to. "Any sign of the others? Aside from Banti?" she asked.

Dante shook his head. "Not that I've seen. Nantu and Kaliha are probably out exploring. And I'm guessing the reporters are working on their pieces."

That's right. Cathryn had said she'd be filing hers later today. Which meant she'd be on her personal time afterward and free to pursue Dante. She scoffed mentally. As if the woman had waited like she said she would. Despite how hungry Sierra had been just a moment ago, the sandwich she'd just taken a bite out of suddenly tasted like sand in her mouth. It went down that way when she swallowed.

Dante took a sip of tea, holding the cup in his hand without setting it down. "Cathryn's the only one who asked me for a quote," he told her before taking another, longer sip.

"A quote?"

"That's right. For her article. She wanted an official palace statement. She came by to see me."

A puzzle piece fell into place in her mind. It appeared very likely that Sierra had come to the wrong conclusion when she'd seen Cathryn leaving Dante's room. So the woman had kept to her stated commitment to professionalism, after all. Sierra's felt a rush of shame for being so quick to judge the other woman. She'd been true to her word. And along with the shame came no small amount of relief that she'd been wrong about her and Dante getting together. Yet.

"Wait, is that why she was in your room yesterday?" Sierra asked before she could stop herself.

Dante's left eyebrow rose about an inch higher. This time, he did set his cup down, so fast and hard some of the tea splashed over the rim and onto the table.

Damn it. She'd given herself away.

"You knew about that?" he asked. "How?"

How in the world could Sierra possibly answer his question without admitting that she'd been upset to see it?

She couldn't think of a single way.

* * *

She'd been jealous. Dante had no doubt about it. Suddenly it made sense—why she'd been acting so angry with him. Not because he'd kissed her that night. But because she thought he might have kissed someone else the very next day.

He wanted to reach for her, to take her hand in his and tell her she was a beautiful little fool. To think for even a moment that he would look at another woman after she'd just left his side.

Truth be told, he'd definitely picked up on some flirtatious vibes from the reporter yesterday. But there was no way he'd even consider reciprocating in any way. Not with Sierra so near. Or even on the same planet.

Wow. That had come out of nowhere. He couldn't examine that sentiment too closely.

It would lead to all sorts of roadways and paths better left unexplored.

Sierra still hadn't answered his question. Dante considered pushing for one before deciding against it. He didn't need an answer to know the truth. So Sierra wasn't as unaffected as she'd claimed to be back in the tree house earlier. Not that it changed anything. After this trip, what would it matter? Neither one of them could do anything about the pull between them. Sierra was wise enough to know it. It wasn't as if he could drop everything once or twice a month and go see her in New York. And she'd already made it perfectly clear that her life was there now. Maybe he could persuade her to come visit Nocera more often than she had since the loss of her best friend.

But then what? What happened when he ultimately had to find a fiancée? Heaven knew he couldn't put it off much longer. What would he do then? Tell Sierra to stop coming around? Not even a possibility.

She deserved better.

As elated as Dante was that Sierra felt enough for him to be jealous of another woman, the simple reality was that there was nothing to be done about it.

So he would be letting it go.

"There's Nantu and Kaliha now," Sierra suddenly announced, standing and waving in the direction of the porch. She looked so relieved at the sight of the other couple, Dante thought she might have somehow summoned them through sheer will. Her smile of greeting when they approached was luminous.

"So glad you're both back safely," Kaliha said as soon as they reached the patio. Her husband nodded in agreement behind her. Soon they'd all taken seats around the table.

"We were very worried when the storm started

and you two were nowhere to be found," Nantu said, helping himself to some tea.

"Thank you for your concern," Sierra told them.

"Apologies for having caused you any alarm," Dante said at the same time. "It was harrowing for a while there, but we managed to find shelter until it passed, in a tree house believe it or not. Then Banti made sure we got back here safely."

Sierra's cheeks turned a bright shade of pink when he'd mentioned the tree house. Was she recalling all that had happened in that shelter, perhaps?

"Well, thank goodness," Kaliha said. "I know the four of us have only just met, but we feel a closeness with you two, I must admit."

Dante couldn't help but feel touched by the woman's words. As crown prince, he had no shortage of people around him every day offering fake platitudes. That Kaliha's words were genuine was clear as the raindrops on the grass nearby.

"We feel that way too," Sierra said, glancing at him for confirmation to speak on his behalf. He gave her a small nod.

Nantu took his wife's hand in his. "It occurred to us that we wanted to ask you something," he said.

"That's right," Kaliha agreed.

"What's that?" Sierra said, just as Dante spoke.

Why were they speaking over each other so often, all of a sudden?

"Our youngest daughter is getting married next month," Kaliha began. "We would very much like you to attend the ceremony. As personal guests of the bride's parents."

An invitation to a wedding was definitely not on his radar. A look at Sierra's open mouth told him she was just as surprised.

"We would hate to impose that way," Sierra immediately began to protest.

"It's not an imposition in at all," Nantu assured her. "You'd be our guests," he repeated.

"But I'm sure your daughter already has her guest list," Sierra said.

Nantu nodded. "Yes, and it continues to grow. Good thing the venue is so large," he added, shaking his head.

"Your daughter and her fiancé are fine with two strangers attending her wedding?" Dante asked. The older couple's ask was unexpected, but hardly unusual. As a member of the royal family, Dante got invited to all sorts of ceremonies—everything from weddings to christenings to bar mitzvahs. Often, he didn't even know the parties personally.

Kaliha chuckled at his question. "Rest assured she's more than fine with it. We've already asked her, of course. And her response about those strangers ran along the lines of just how much she'd be thrilled to have the Nocera crown prince and the most anticipated designer in the world of fashion there to share in her special day."

Sierra cleared her throat, leaned forward. "I'm so honored, Nantu," she said, and turned her gaze to the other woman. "Kaliha. But I'm not sure how I would manage to come back here in a month. My schedule is stretched enough as it is."

"That's the best part, dear," Kaliha said, clasping her hands in front of her. "It just so happens that her husband to be is a Wall Street banker. She'll be getting married in Manhattan. You won't even have to travel anywhere, Sierra."

Sierra glanced at Dante, her eyes wide as if seeking his help. Darned if he could come up with a way to do so. The wedding would be taking place in Sierra's figurative back yard. How could she possibly say no?

Her tight smile told him she couldn't come up with an answer either. "Then it would be a privilege," she finally said. "Thank you for the honor of inviting us."

A server appeared to ask them if they needed anything.

"In fact we would," Nantu answered. "Something chilled and sparkling, please. To celebrate that the four of us will be seeing one another again in a few weeks for a most festive occasion."

That settled it then. If Sierra would be attending, then so would he. Suddenly, it appeared he had something to look forward to.

There was no way she was going to get any sleep tonight. It didn't help that she'd retired to her room ridiculously early to avoid running into Dante.

Her mind kept replaying the day's events. The scare with Banti's brother, the storm that came out of nowhere. Being stranded several feet above ground with Dante. Falling asleep only to awaken in his lap and what had almost happened afterward.

And the coup de grâce with the way it all ended. With the knowledge that she'd be seeing him again in New York at a lavish wedding of all places.

Sierra wasn't sure how her heart was supposed to handle that. Once she left Africa, she figured it would take all her effort to try to forget him and the time they'd shared together down here. So much for that plan. Her heart would hardly get a chance to recover before she would have to see him again.

With a frustrated sigh, she pulled apart the canopy above her bed and crawled off the mattress. She needed some air. Grabbing the bug lotion from the bathroom vanity, she lathered a thick layer on her skin then threw on a pair of leggings and a long-sleeved top.

Going out this late was probably asking for trouble in the form of a thousand bug bites, even with the smelly repellant on. But she was going stir-crazy in her room with her mind racing like a Thoroughbred at a derby.

Stepping out onto the porch, Sierra sucked in a deep breath of air. Apparently she wasn't the only one roaming about. A faint light glowed from inside the dining room. Curious, she made her way toward the entrance and through the lobby.

She was right. There was someone else awake. Cathryn sat at one of the long tables, an open bag of chips, a frosty bottle of beer and an open paperback in front of her.

Sierra debated turning around and leaving her to it when Cathryn suddenly looked up. A smile appeared on her face, inviting Sierra to walk farther into the room.

"You couldn't sleep either?" she asked rhetorically.

Cathryn shook her head. "I'm always too ramped up after filing a piece. This is how I wind down and celebrate meeting my deadline." She gestured to the items sitting in front of her. "Join me."

"I don't want to intrude on your celebration."

Cathryn waved a hand in dismissal of her comment. "Nonsense, I'd love the company." She reached for a second frosty bottle in a small cooler by her leg, twisted the cap then pushed it across the table to Sierra.

Sierra pulled out the chair opposite and sat. There was no good way to bring up the question at the forefront of her mind. So she decided to just blurt it out. "So, now that you've finished writing the article, do you plan on talking to Dante?"

Cathryn took a swig of her beer. "Yeah, I've changed my mind about that, actually."

Something loosened in the pit of Sierra's stomach. She released the breath she'd been holding. "Oh?"

"Yeah. I went to see him about a quote for the article and decided pretty much right away that it wasn't a good idea to start anything."

Huh. "Why's that?"

Cathryn shrugged, brought the bottle back to her lips, speaking before taking another swig. "The vibes were off. We weren't really meshing. I can tell right away when a man isn't interested, you know what I mean?"

Sierra couldn't help but be impressed with the reporter. Cathryn wasn't afraid to go after what she wanted but knew when to say when. Exactly the type of woman Sierra would want as a friend.

"I think any man would be lucky to have you come on to him. Dante's loss," she said, surprising herself.

Cathryn tipped the bottle head in her direction. "Hey, thanks for saying so."

"You're welcome."

A sly smile spread over Cathryn's mouth. "You know, your name came up a lot during my conversation with Dante."

Her ears began to hum at Cathryn's announcement. "It did?"

"Sure did. It was one of the reasons I knew to back off. And also the reason I asked you first about him before I did anything."

Sierra rubbed her forehead. The woman was too observant by half. She supposed that's what made for a good journalist. "Things are complicated," she answered. "Between Dante and me. And after this trip ends in two days, we'll be on our separate ways and off to separate lives." Until she would have to see him again at the wedding in New York.

Cathryn's eyes narrowed. "That may be so, but it doesn't look all that complicated from where I'm sitting."

"He used to be married to my dearest friend in the world."

Cathryn whistled out a breath. "That's right. Now that you mention it, I remember from my research that the person accompanying the prince on this trip was someone with whom he had some sort of connection. His sister-in-law, or something."

The description was close enough. She and Rula had been like sisters, after all.

"It must have slipped my mind," Cathryn added.

That said quite a bit about Sierra's relative importance as a member of this mission. One of the journalists here to cover it had barely made note of her until just now. It just reaffirmed what Sierra already knew, that she had no real business in Dante's world in any kind of permanent way. If Rula were here, she'd be sure to be noticed. She would behave the way a future queen would behave. Rula wasn't the type of person who ever slipped someone's mind.

"You're right," Cathryn said after a pause. "I stand corrected. That is complicated." She polished off the rest of the beer and set the bottle down. "But maybe it doesn't have to be?"

* * *

Sierra made her way back to her cabin, her thoughts a jumble of confusion. Cathryn had no idea. Things between her and Dante couldn't get much more complicated. They had a history as childhood friends. He'd been married to her closest friend, whom they'd both lost. There'd always been an undercurrent of tension between them. Tension that had come perilously close to the surface during this trip. Soon, he would be on the search for a suitable wife in order to be better positioned to take his place on the throne when the time came.

It didn't get much more complicated than that.

Speak of the devil, she found him outside the door to her room as she approached from the other side of the shared porch. He lifted his hand to knock then dropped it when he saw her approaching. His smile widened into a grin. "There you are."

"Hey, Dante. Something I can do for you?"

The grin faltered ever so slightly at her lack of enthusiasm at finding him there. What exactly was he expecting?

He lifted the object he was holding. A sweaty bottle. "Thought you might be up for a nightcap."

Sierra stepped past him to her door. Of course she would be up for a nightcap, given who was asking. But it was late, her emotions were in turmoil. And Dante looked so devastatingly handsome in a deep blue button-down shirt that brought out the steel gray of his eyes, and khaki pants that fit his long legs like they were tailored for him. Which of course they were. Her will-power could only be able to withstand so much.

"I just had a nightcap," she told him, knowing full well how rude and dismissive she sounded. "With Cathryn."

He eyebrows drew close together. "The reporter?"

She nodded. "That's right."

"Oh." Disappointment washed over his features. "Maybe we can just talk then."

Sierra wanted to turn him down. She really did. It would be the smartest and most prudent course. But she couldn't do it. She wanted to talk to him, wanted to have one more night in his company.

That made her all sorts of a fool.

She stepped inside her room and motioned for him to follow. The grin reappeared above his chin, and she couldn't help the smile that lifted her own lips.

He reached for her hand then, and Sierra made herself not react to the jolt of electricity that shot through her arm and into her lower belly at the contact. Why did she react in this manner whenever this man touched her? Even in the most innocent way?

"To what do I owe this visit?" she asked, pulling her hand away and dropping onto the mattress of her bed. She curled one leg under the other.

Dante set the unopened bottle on the coffee table and pulled over the chair from the sitting area so that he was about a foot away from Sierra. Thank heavens he hadn't attempted to sit down next to her. Her mind filled with images of where that scenario might have led, and she had to force herself to focus on Dante's face.

"I wanted to run something by you," he told her.

Something about his tone and his demeanor sent alarm bells ringing in her head. She got the distinct impression she wasn't going to like whatever was about to come out of Dante's mouth.

"What's that?"

"I was thinking, Noccra, and particularly the Angilera palace grounds, just haven't been the same since you left the kingdom."

The alarm bells grew louder. "Um…thanks?"

"More selfishly, I have to confess to the fact that I miss having you around."

Huh.

Dante continued, "You've always been such

a big part of my life. It's felt so much emptier after your move."

Sierra's breath hitched in her throat, and a nervous knot tightened in her center. Where exactly was Dante going with this?

He leaned over, braced his elbows on his knees. "Lots of fashion designers have more than one city where they're located. Many of them have fashion houses all over the world."

What in heaven's name was he possibly getting at? "Those would be actual fashion houses, Dante. Run by titans of the industry. I'm merely an assistant designer working my way up. Big difference."

He winked at her conspiratorially. "But you don't have to be."

Sierra crossed her arms in front of her chest, some foolish part of her heart deflating with disappointment. "Maybe you should just come right out and say what it is you're getting at."

"What if you could be the lead designer working out of your own empire. I would back you. Nocera could become another power player in the fashion industry. And you would be in charge of the launch."

There it was. Sierra could hardly believe what she was hearing. For an insane moment, she'd thought maybe he was about to admit to something deeper. How downright foolish of her.

"So you're offering me a job. Is that it?"

He leaned back against the chair. "I suppose I am. What do you say?"

She might have laughed if it wasn't so darn heartbreaking. Dante wanted her back in Nocera with him. But he couldn't just say so. He couldn't admit that he felt anything for her. She could only think of one reason.

He still hadn't gotten over Rula's loss.

So he was offering her a job working for the kingdom in order to have her near. Sierra would be a crutch until he could find the proper replacement for his perished wife, which Sierra clearly wasn't.

And what would become of such an arrangement when he eventually remarried? Was she to turn into a fixture in the background then? A fragment of his former life?

Without giving herself a chance to think, she blurted out the question that had been plaguing her subconscious. "Why do you never talk about her?"

"Talk about who?" He had to know the answer to that. Sierra got the impression he was just buying time.

"Rula. You never so much as mention her name. That afternoon with Banti, you said your wife would be a hard act to follow."

He blinked at her in confusion. "What I'm offering you now has nothing to do with Rula."

"I think it does."

His gaze narrowed on her face. "I could ask you the same question."

Touché, dear prince. Her answer might have surprised him. That her hesitation to speak of Rula had a lot to the with the guilt she carried regarding her friend's loss. Guilt that Sierra might not have been there when Rula had needed her, pursuing a dream in New York rather than being available to her friend. All because she'd had to get away rather than watch Dante and Rula begin their married lives together.

Dante rubbed his forehead then began to speak, apparently giving up on waiting for Sierra to answer. "Things between Rula and me, they were complicated, Sierra."

There was that word again. So many complications between them. How would they ever get past it all?

She couldn't see a way. Slowly, she rose off the mattress. "Thank you for the job offer, but I'm not interested."

Dante rose, his lips tight, his eyes pleading. "Sierra..."

She didn't wait for him to continue, went to

the door instead and opened it. "I think I'd like to retire for the evening."

Dante washed his hand across his face then strode to the open doorway. He turned back.

"Sierra," he repeated.

But she was done listening. "Good night, Dante." *And goodbye*, she added silently.

CHAPTER TEN

Four weeks later

DANTE SLAMMED THE drawer of his desk hard enough that several items fell off the top and a priceless painting on the wall behind him dropped to a slant. Biting out a curse, he looked up to find his mother entering his office.

"Is everything all right, dear?" she asked.

No. The answer to her question was a big, fat resounding no. Nothing was all right. Everything was irritating him. Even a simple email about a slight delay in shipping due to a canal backup had him irritated and ready to snap.

Of course, he wasn't going to tell Maman any of that.

"Why do you ask?" he asked instead.

His mother tilted her head, her lips drawing tight. "Please don't be a smart a—" She caught herself before finishing. "Don't be a smart aleck," she amended. "Let's not pretend you haven't been in an absolute terror of a mood since returning from the safari."

Dante pinched the bridge of his nose. "I apologize, Maman. I've just had a lot on my mind."

That was a lie. He'd only had one thing on his mind. Sierra. In fact, he couldn't stop thinking about her.

"Well, I can only hope this trip to New York will perhaps lighten your mood. Am I to understand Sierra will be there?"

"That's correct." There was no way to explain to his mother that Sierra was the source of his torment.

"That's good then," his mother said with a smile. "She's always had a way of brightening your disposition. It's a shame she lives so far away. Perhaps you can convince her to come back to Nocera somehow."

Dante studied his mother's face, the understanding in her eyes. *She knew.* And perhaps she'd always known. He should know better than to underestimate the woman. But the reality was what it was. Sierra had gone back to her life in New York without so much as a second glance at him when they'd landed back on American soil. What choice had he had but to jet back to Nocera alone?

"Why would I do that, Maman?"

His mother reached across the desk, patted his forearm. "Oh, son, I think you know why."

Dante leaned back in his chair. No use pretending he didn't know what she meant. "I'm afraid there's no use. I have responsibilities. I need to put Nocera first. And Sierra's decided that her new life is in New York. She's moved on. The same way I need to."

His mother squinted her eyes at him. If he didn't know better, he might say she was disappointed in his words. Or maybe she was just disappointed in *him*.

"Have you asked her that, son? Or are you just assuming? If it's the latter, then I'd have to say that's rather arrogant of you."

Arrogant? Of course that wasn't it. Was it? "There's nothing for her here. She's made that quite clear."

"Are you sure there's nothing? Nothing she might consider a life change for? Or no one who might possibly make her change her mind?"

Dante's aggravation skyrocketed once more. As much as he loved and respected her, his mother didn't know what she was talking about. "Sierra had every opportunity to tell me so if she felt that way." In fact, he'd given her an ideal opportunity to return to the kingdom that was her home, and she'd turned him down flat.

Maman nodded slowly. "You're right. She did.

And you had every opportunity to tell her how you felt. Instead, you made her some kind of job offer."

Well, when she put it that way…

Dante cursed under his breath. His mother was right, as much as he wanted to deny it. What Maman just described was the very definition of arrogance.

"Maybe it's time to forgive yourself, son."

Dante jolted upright at his mother's words. So unexpected, so jarring. "What's that supposed to mean?"

Maman gave him a smile full of affection. And sympathy. She reached over and patted his cheek. "I think you know the answer to that question."

Yet Dante was still pondering his mother's words long after she'd left the room. Self-forgiveness hardly came easy. Certainly not in his case. Where would he even begin? Out of duty, he'd married the woman he'd been expected to wed. It had resulted in tragedy. Rula had eventually and gradually decided she wanted more than a loveless marriage. She'd made it known to him in many subtle and not so subtle ways.

Dante had never been able to bring himself to even try. Maybe if he had, she wouldn't have felt the need to flee. He'd driven her away. For that, he had no one else to blame but himself.

Dante swore out loud and leaned his head back to stare at the ceiling. Maman knew all this.

Still, she'd said what she had. Her words echoed once again in his head.

Maybe it's time to forgive yourself...

"I can't believe you've scored an invite to the most talked about wedding in Manhattan this year."

Camille was much more excited than Sierra herself was about her plans for the evening. Sierra adjusted the hem of her silk dress and slipped into the matching navy stilettos. "Neither can I." And she couldn't wait for it to be over.

The butterflies in her stomach multiplied with each turn of the second hand on the vintage watch that she'd scored from the pop-up market in SoHo. Each revolution on the clockface meant that Sierra was that much closer to seeing Dante again. She had no idea what she would say when she did. The safari seemed like years ago, another lifetime perhaps.

Did he think about her as often as she thought about him? Highly unlikely. And no use dwelling on.

"Thanks for coming by to let me borrow these," she said now to Camille, toying with the diamond drop earrings the young model's latest boyfriend had gifted her. They were something Sierra would never be able to afford.

"Sure thing. It gave me a chance to watch you get ready." She eyed her up and down. "You look amazing. The prince is going to go gaga at the sight of you."

Sierra had to laugh at that. Camille had such a way with words. Part of her wanted desperately for the other woman's prediction about Dante to be true. Another part was scared to death at the prospect.

Would they be seated together? It made sense. They'd been invited by the bride's parents. Sierra assumed there would be specific tables for such guests.

A thought suddenly occurred to her that had a wave of horror crashing through her core. What if Dante wouldn't be coming alone? What if he was bringing a date? One of the many possible women who would make a great candidate to be the next queen. Nausea rolled around her stomach at the thought. How in the world would Sierra sit there and watch him accompany another woman into the hall? Watch him dance with her, hold her in his arms, the way he'd held her the night of the bonfire.

"What's the matter?" Camille asked, concern etched in her eyes. "You've just gone pale as a ghost."

"Nothing," she lied. "I guess I just haven't eaten enough today." That last part was true enough. She'd been too nervous to eat. Or to do much of anything, for that matter.

Her fingers still stung from all the times she'd pricked herself with a needle today during fittings due to her distraction.

"Saving room for the wedding dinner, huh?" Camille said. "I heard it's being catered by none other than Simone Billieu of the Parisian."

If Camille thought that name was supposed mean something to Sierra, she was sadly mistaken. Her lack of appetite these past few days had nothing to do with the menu of a distinguished chef and everything to do with seeing Dante again.

She really needed this wedding to be over so that she could get back to her life.

A life where she could finally put thoughts of Dante Angilera out of her mind once and for all.

She sensed him before she saw him. The air in the banquet hall seemed to stir. The rumble of voices grew a fraction quieter. Heads began to turn in the direction of the entryway. Leave it to Dante to make an entrance. Sierra braced herself to turn and look his way. Her breath caught in her throat when she did. Out of respect for his hosts and following tradition, he was wearing his official uniform—a military jacket in a deep rich burgundy with all his honors and medals pinned to one side of his chest and the crest of the house of Angilera on the other. Black pants with precise, razor-sharp pleats, and polished black shoes completed a look that only a prince like Dante could wear.

Sierra hadn't seen him at all at the ceremony earlier. He must have made a relatively quick entrance then sat in the back of the room in order to avoid drawing any attention to himself.

Now, he looked like something out of a painting that might be hanging in one of the finest museums in Europe. He looked like the king he was destined to become.

"Yowza!" came an impressed cry from a female voice somewhere in her vicinity. As good a reaction as any. Heaven knew she herself had been rendered speechless at the sight of him.

"Oh, my God," a different voice nearby said. "He's coming this way."

That he was. Sierra's heart pounded in her chest as he made his way across the hall. When he looked up and his gaze zeroed in on her, she thought her heart would stop altogether. The man she'd been on safari with had been casual and relaxed. Here, he was the epitome of regal. This was the side of Dante that had always intimidated her, made her feel like an alien in the world he inhabited. It was a stark reminder of what she could never be and where she would never fit in.

He was at the table in a few long strides, most of the eyes in the room following his path. He smiled when he saw her and Sierra was grateful she was sitting down; her knees had gone weak. Actually, every joint in her body felt as if it might have turned to Jell-O.

"Good evening, Sierra," he said, as if they'd just left each other's company the other day as opposed to several weeks ago. Pulling out the empty chair next to her, he sat down.

Sierra cleared her throat and forced her mouth to work. "Dante, how lovely to see you again."

So formal, but it was all she could come up with. If he had brought somebody with him, they were nowhere to be seen at the moment. Maybe he had and the woman was merely in the ladies' room powdering her nose, or preparing to make her own entrance. But that made no sense. Any woman in her right mind would want to step into any room on Dante's arm. Still, Sierra had to know for sure before she could resume any kind of normal breath. "Are you here alone?" she asked, before she could lose her nerve and find out the answer the hard way.

He lifted an eyebrow, clearly surprised by the

question. "Yes," he answered, then after a pause added, "And you?"

"Yes."

Was it her imagination, or had he just clenched his fists until hearing her answer?

The bride and groom walked in at that moment to thunderous applause. The bridal party followed, including Nantu and Kaliha. They all took their seats at the head table.

Several waiters appeared from various corners wheeling carts full of food.

"Nantu and Kaliha look like the quintessential example of proud parents," Dante remarked. "They're both beaming."

"They are," she agreed. "And how are your parents?" she asked. "The king and queen."

"They're doing well. They send their regards."

"I'm glad to hear it. You must give them my best when you return." God, she hated this small talk. They were speaking to each other like strangers. While a few weeks ago, she'd been on this man's lap while clad in nothing but a thin tunic.

Don't go there.

She had to force that image out of her mind before her cheeks turned the color of the tomato in the salad that had just been placed before her.

Sierra could barely pick at the food on her

plate, despite having not eaten all day. Her stomach was simply in too many knots.

If Dante noticed she wasn't eating, he didn't comment on it.

By the time their plates were cleared away and the bride and groom moved to the dance floor for their first dance, Sierra's pulse still had yet to slow.

It didn't help that Dante leaned over to whisper in her ear. "You look amazing."

She had to swallow the lump that formed in her throat at his compliment.

He continued before she'd even begun to recover. "Like I told you once already, you clean up really well."

"Thank you," Sierra managed to say, trying hard not to follow the path his words were leading her down, back to Valhali and the afternoon of the storm. "You don't look so bad yourself."

He stood suddenly, extended his hand to her. "In that case, perhaps you'll grant me the honor of this dance."

Oh, no. In alarm, Sierra glanced at the dance floor to discover that other couples had joined the bride and groom there, moving along to a slow ballad.

The prospect of being in Dante's arms again, moving with him, feeling his warmth against her skin—she wasn't sure she could handle it.

But what choice did she have? She couldn't exactly say no while he stood with his hand out to her. She'd already hesitated a second too long; the others at the table had begun to stare.

Bracing herself with a steadying breath, she stood and placed her hand in his, then followed him to the dance floor.

Maybe he shouldn't have put her on the spot that way when he'd asked her to dance. But Dante couldn't take another minute of sitting so close to her, inhaling that vanilla and rose perfume of hers. The need to touch her and to hold her pulsed like shots of electricity through his system.

The way she'd hesitated had sent a figurative dagger through his heart. Now that she was in his arms again, he wasn't sure he'd ever be able to let her go again.

He could feel the heat of her skin through her silk dress. The familiar scent of her shampoo had him longing to nuzzle his face into her hair and inhale deeply. Was he imagining her slight tremble? Did he dare hope she was as affected as he was right this moment? If so, he would guess she was doing her best to try to hide it.

Well, there was no hiding his own reaction at having her in his arms again. He'd missed her. More than he would have ever anticipated. He thanked his lucky stars that Nantu and Kaliha had made this meeting between them possible. He wasn't going to let the opportunity go to waste. When the song ended, Sierra immediately stepped out of his arms, and it felt like a bucket of ice water splashed over him.

"I could use a drink, if you don't mind," she said, not quite meeting his eyes. If he didn't know better, he might think she was being shy with him. That wouldn't do. Not at all. Not given what he had to say to her as soon as he got her alone.

"Sure, I'll get it for you."

When he returned to the table with two glasses of champagne and handed one to her, Sierra appeared still unwilling to make eye contact. A rush of exasperation flushed through his system.

Enough.

He waited silently until she finished her drink, his patience hanging by a thread. When she was done, he pushed his chair back and stood, holding his hand out to her once more.

Sierra looked up at him finally but immediately shook her head. "I don't think I'm up for another dance just yet."

"No. I don't mean another dance. Can we go somewhere to talk? Alone?"

She blinked in surprise. Once and then again.

Still, she didn't stand. For one excruciating moment, Dante thought she might turn him down. Finally, after several awkward beats, she pushed her chair back, rose to her feet and took his hand.

He led her toward the exit. Otto immediately started following them. Dante gestured to him, a movement of his hand so small it was almost imperceptible. But the bodyguard got the message and immediately stopped, though he didn't look terribly happy about it.

Soon, the two of them were out the main doors, down the hallway and to a doorway with a bright red exit sign above it. They found themselves at the foot of a stairway that went up several flights.

Sierra smoothed down the skirt of her dress, as if the fabric was the most interesting thing on the planet and required all her attention. "Well, this certainly is private, Dante."

He took a steadying breath before speaking. "Sierra, look at me."

It took her a few beats, but she eventually did as he asked. Finally. When her eyes met his, Dante hated that he couldn't read what he saw in their depths. However, there was no turning back now. In for a penny and all that.

"I have a confession to make," he began.

Her tongue darted out to swipe at her bottom

lip, and Dante lost his focus for a moment. He wrangled himself back to the matter at hand with no small amount of effort.

"Yes?"

"I missed you. I need you to know that. There hasn't been a day since we parted that I haven't missed you. The way I went about asking you to come back to Nocera in Valhali went all wrong. I should have thought out better what I was going to say and how I wanted to say it."

She sucked in a breath. "Which was what, exactly?"

Couldn't she see it in his eyes? Didn't she understand how hard it was to speak the words? "That I wanted you to come back with me to Nocera. That I needed you by my side." The rest of it was on the tip of his tongue—that he loved her and always had. But the dark torment behind her eyes kept him from saying the words out loud.

She squeezed her eyes shut, and Dante felt the need to hold his breath until she responded. Which took an agonizingly long time.

"Oh, Dante," was all she said.

"Sierra, say something." As much as he loved the sound of his name on her lips, he needed more from her right now. Much more.

"What would you have me say?" she asked, her voice a low whisper that sent shards of glass through his heart. The heart he'd just laid at her feet.

"You don't know?" he asked. "Nothing comes to mind?"

Like maybe that you missed me too? Or how about that you've been thinking about me? Or maybe you could throw me a paltry bone along the lines of "I'll call you sometime."

At this point, he would take it. He would take anything.

But Sierra didn't seem inclined to offer him anything.

When she opened her eyes again, Dante felt a small sprig of hope when he saw the wetness in them. If she was on the verge of crying, surely that had to mean she felt something for him. Sierra crushed that hope with her next words.

"I'm sorry, but I can't say the words you seem to want to hear."

The air left his lungs like a pricked balloon. What a fool he was. Standing here declaring his love for her only to be rebuffed.

She went on, rubbing her forehead. "If you'll excuse me, I'm feeling rather light-headed."

He couldn't help the concern that washed over him, despite what was happening between them at the moment. "Are you all right?"

She moved out of his reach and another stabbing sensation pierced his gut.

"I'm fine," she said. "I just haven't eaten much today, and I shouldn't have drunk the champagne so quickly. I think I'll pay my respects to our hosts and make it an earlier night than expected."

All right. If that's what she wanted. "I'll come with you, see you home."

She held a hand up. "No, that won't be necessary. Please, you've come all this way to attend this wedding. I'd hate for you to leave on my account."

Right. As if he could spend one more minute here at this party given that she was about to leave.

"Sierra, just let me see you home. I just want to make sure you get there safely."

She squared her shoulders, lifted her chin in a stubborn movement that left no room for question. "Dante, please don't follow me. There's no need. I know my way around this city. I'll be fine by myself. I live here. Permanently."

Her double meaning couldn't have been more clear than if she'd etched it on his chest with a knife.

Without another word, she turned on her heel and stepped out the door.

Leaving him standing there, with no other choice but to watch her go.

Sierra was on the second box of tissues an hour after she'd left the banquet hall. Not too many sheets left in this one. Still, the tears would not stop falling. Her heart was shattered, irreparably damaged. Dante would never forgive her, would never understand that she'd merely done what she had to do in that stairwell. She couldn't be what he needed; it wasn't in her makeup to be any kind of queen. The very idea was petrifying. He would have realized it soon enough, the first time she fell flat on her face at a royal event. Or when she made a fool of herself because she didn't know what fork to use at a state dinner.

By then it would be too late.

Dante knew it too. That's why he couldn't say the three words to her that might have had her giving in to her feelings for him. He hadn't been able to say them back in Valhali, and he hadn't been able to say them tonight.

I love you.

No. They both knew Sierra could never be Dante's queen. And what was the other option? A meaningless fling? Some type of shallow relationship that would need to end when he did move on to someone more suitable?

Sierra couldn't survive that. She couldn't watch him walk down the aisle with another woman, stand idly by and nurse her wounds when he eventually had children with someone else.

The mere thought had her gasping for air.

Finally all cried out, she fell asleep where she sat on the couch, sheer heartbreak and exhaustion eventually gaining the upper hand.

It was Rula who woke her up. Somehow back from the dead.

Her dear friend's voice rang clear in her head. Though the word she kept repeating made no sense: *journey.*

Sierra jolted up in her seat, waking with a start. The neon lights outside her window had dimmed, the street was quiet. A glance at her watch told her she'd been asleep for three hours.

That was the most realistic dream she'd ever had. As if Rula had been right there in the room with her. A stab of longing pierced her chest. If only Rula was really still here. Sierra would give anything to seek her advice, ask her what she might do to ease the anguish. Although that notion was downright nonsensical given the reason Sierra would need to ask in the first place.

Rula's familiar voice echoed through her head again.

Journey.

Why was she hearing what she was? Her mind had to be playing tricks on her. Of course Rula wasn't trying to tell her anything from beyond. And even if that were somehow miraculously possible, why would her friend be referring to a journey?

Sierra gave her head a shake. Her mind was simply trying to call up the memories of the journey she'd been on with Dante. That had to be what the silly dream was about.

But the voice persisted.

Journal.

Not journey.

Sierra sucked in a breath. She could no longer deny that something was trying to give her some sort of message. Even if it was in her own mind.

Journal.

The word triggered an idea in the back of her head. Sierra had been given a box of Rula's things upon her passing. Her parents weren't exactly the sentimental kind or much of the grieving type. They'd offered the personal belongings to Rula's best friend, uninterested in the sentimentality of knickknacks.

Sierra hadn't had it in her to go through the box two years ago in the depths of grief. Was there a chance Rula had kept a journal? Sierra had never considered herself a very spiritual person. But she couldn't shake the sense that something, or someone, wanted her to go find out the answer. Without giving herself a chance to overthink, Sierra stood and walked to her closet. Using a stool, she reached to the back of the top shelf until she felt the velvet cover of the box that held her friend's things.

As soon as she removed the ribbon and lifted the lid, her eyes began to flood again. Photos of the two of them as children, riding horses, eating ice cream, splashing in the crystal blue water in the ocean at one of Nocera's more popular beaches. Another picture of Rula in her wedding dress. Yet another one where she was having a tiara placed on her head by the king.

Surprisingly, there were none of her and Dante together. Or any of Dante at all, for that matter. Maybe the royal couple wanted to keep those at the palace. It made sense; it was the only logical explanation.

Sierra looked through the other items, removing them carefully and setting them aside—everything from theater tickets to newspaper clippings, to press announcements. Nothing really of value but obviously full of sentiment. Finally, at the very bottom, Sierra found a thick notebook bound in a buttery soft leather cover. Her hands shook as she lifted it. Judging by the outside, it definitely appeared to be some type of journal or diary.

Sierra almost dropped it right back in the box to seal everything up again. A journal was meant to be confidential, wasn't it? A way to vent and purge some of a person's most private thoughts. She couldn't bring herself to read Rula's most intimate writings, couldn't intrude on her late friend's privacy that way.

Before she put it away, Sierra granted herself a small allowance and thumbed the edge of the pages like a deck of cards, just to have a look at the handwriting. Rula had had the most beautiful penmanship, each letter almost a work of art.

Then she saw it, blinked to make sure she wasn't imagining things. But it was unmistakable. Sierra's name was written at the top line of every page.

Her friend may have been writing in a journal, but she'd been writing to Sierra.

CHAPTER ELEVEN

DANTE STUDIED THE glass of amber liquid he'd poured about two hours ago but had barely sipped. As much as he wanted to obliterate the pain of the past few hours by drowning himself in drink, he knew in the end that was only prolonging his suffering.

The sooner he got it over with, the better. Then he could move on and do what he should have done in the first place—go forward with his life and do his best to forget Sierra Compari ever existed.

And somewhere along the way, he would have to forget what a fool of himself he'd made over her.

Ha! Easier said than done.

Suddenly the frustration and disappointment of the past few hours became too much. All the weeks of missing her, wanting to somehow deny that he was. Followed by days where he'd thought maybe if he professed his feelings, she would confess to hers. Only to have it blow up in his face. Rather than take another sip, he instead flung the drink against the hanging mirror with such force that both the mirror and the glass shattered.

He felt only marginally better.

And now he had a mess to clean up on top of everything else. First thing first. He wasn't going to waste another minute pining for a woman who either didn't want him or didn't want to acknowledge that she did.

Either way, he was ready to move on. Making his way to the desk in the corner, he fired up his laptop and began composing an email to his personal secretary.

Time to get the ball moving on his future.

Sierra hadn't left the floor of her closet since walking in there an hour ago. A cursory glance through Rula's notebook confirmed her suspicions. Her friend had been journaling in the form of letters to Sierra.

They hadn't been particularly close as adults, something Sierra would always regret now. But Sierra had always been the one Rula had confided in with her deepest secrets. And this notebook had a fair share of those.

Rubbing her eyes, Sierra read the first page once more, somehow keeping the tears at bay this time.

Dearest Sierra,
One of these days I'm going to rip all these pages out and send them to you. Or maybe I'll just send you the entire book all at once. But right now I just need to get everything down and out of my system.

You see, my dear sweet friend, I've made such a mess of things. I've realized too late that the life I pursued for so long wasn't the life I wanted after all. I married for status, for prestige, for a title. I married for all the wrong reasons and not the only right one... the only reason that matters.

My husband is a good man. I do love him. But I didn't really know what passionate love was until I met *him*. The man I should have waited for and married instead.

Sierra sniffled onto the sleeve of her sweater before she could continue. The rest of the pages were variations of the same theme. Rula had fallen for one of Dante's closest advisers. Dante had to have known. But he'd never said anything to her. Had kept his wife's confidence even after her death. Not just from her, but from the entire world.

Sierra's heart twisted as she remembered the fight back in Valhali. She'd been so unfair to

Dante, the things she'd said. The accusation she'd hurled at him. Still, he'd kept silent about Rula's betrayal. He hadn't so much as defended himself.

Despite all that, he'd shown up tonight and swallowed his pride for her. And what had she done in response? Dismissed him like he was an errant admirer she didn't have time for. It was almost too much to bear to think about. Yet another sob escaped her throat as she recalled his stricken expression when she'd simply turned away and left him in that stairwell, admonishing him for daring to ask about taking her home. How would she ever explain that she'd only done all of it to protect her own heart? Dante had every right not to give her the time of day after tonight.

She'd been such a fool.

Sierra turned her focus back to the journal in her lap. The last page was of the most consequence. Sierra's heart broke for the woman she'd once viewed as close as a sister while she reread it.

Dearest Sierra,
We've decided it's time. Ronaldo and I are leaving for the Italian Alps first thing to-morrow. We're going to take a few days to

decide our next course of action and just spend time together.

I'm so excited to leave. I know this is the right decision for everyone. I'm certain Dante knows. He has to. He's a smart man who'll put two and two together. I think he will recover quickly.

You see, I don't think he's fallen in love with me any more than I had with him. He's handsome, of course. With everything going for him. He's a prince! But ours was a match made out of convenience. I think it's best for both Dante and I that it be dissolved.

I'll be mailing you these pages as soon as I return. To give you a chance to learn it all before we can finally meet face-to-face once more, and you can celebrate my new life with me and you finally meet the man who's stolen my heart.

That was the last entry. Sierra closed the book gently and held it tight to her chest. Rula would never return from the Alps, would never get a chance to mail these pages to her.

But Sierra had managed to get them all the same. If Sierra knew her friend at all, Rula had somehow made sure of it.

Sierra continued to sit in her closet with her

back against the wall until the bright rays of the sun shone through the large pane window. The irony of it all wasn't lost on her.

Rula had prepared her whole life to marry the crown prince so that she could become queen. Ultimately, it hadn't made her happy. Judging by her own words, she hadn't found such happiness until she'd found the man she really loved. It had ended in tragedy instead. Her dear friend had discovered too late that titles and crowns weren't important. In the end, love was the only thing that mattered.

A hiccup escaped Sierra's throat, and she finally stood on wobbly, shaky legs. She felt raw and spent. But there wasn't any time to lose. It may be too late for Rula, but Sierra still had a chance. Rula wouldn't want her to waste that chance. Rula would want her to be happy. His former wife would want Dante to be happy too.

She just hoped Dante still believed that Sierra might be the path to that happiness for him. After the way she'd reacted to him at the wedding, she wouldn't be surprised if he'd hopped on his jet and returned to Nocera already. Dante wasn't the type of man who swallowed his pride at all let alone twice. Was it at all possible he might do so for her?

Only one way to find out.

The words echoed through her head. She

couldn't even be sure if it was her own voice she heard. Or if it was Rula's.

His secretary phoned him bright and early the next morning. Dante wasn't surprised. He'd been expecting the man's reaction to the email he'd sent last night.

"Am I to understand, Your Highness, that you would like this visit scheduled as early as next week?"

"That's correct. If the sultan and his daughter are available, please clear my schedule so that I may fly out as soon as they're ready to receive me." Dante had no doubt they would indeed be available. The sultan had been trying to get his daughter to meet him for the better part of a year now. Dante figured they were a good start on his fiancée-finding mission. A logical and thought-out approach to what needed to be done. He should have done it months ago, had just been putting off the inevitable.

"That would mean you're canceling some very important meetings, Your Highness. Are you sure?"

Dante pinched the bridge of his nose. He really needed his agenda to move forward before he had a chance to change his mind. "Yes, I'm certain, Duvall. This takes precedence over everything else."

"Consider it done."

Good. That was one check mark off the to-do list. Dante thanked the man then ended the call. Now he had to get ready for a long day of travel. It had been nice seeing Nantu and Kaliha and meeting their daughter and her husband last night. But in all other respects, this trip had been a waste of his precious time.

Not to mention the blow he'd taken to his pride. And his heart.

Served him right for going against everything he believed in and taking a chance.

Dante had just stepped out of the shower and toweled off when the knock sounded on his hotel room door. Throwing on a pair of sports shorts, he ran to answer. Room service was early by an entire hour.

But it wasn't a hotel employee across the threshold when he flung the door open.

"Sierra?"

She smiled at him shyly. "Good morning, Dante. Hope I'm not intruding."

What in the world was she doing here? After what she'd said last night and the way she'd hightailed it away from him, she was the last person he'd been expecting to see.

Just when he'd thought he had his future figured out, when he'd finally made the decision to get past this stage in his life and had finally acted on it, here she was at his door. Would he ever understand women? This one in particular vexed him like no other.

"How did you know which hotel I'd be at?"

She ducked her head. "I called your mother."

He almost laughed at how childlike that sounded. But the situation was too serious for laughter. Even now, he couldn't help but notice how beautiful she looked. Her hair was wet, her cheeks glowing from the exertion of rushing uptown. Her lips were swollen and red, as if she'd been chewing on them in concentration. He knew from their days on safari that she only did that when she was sketching. It took every ounce of will he had not to reach for her and take those plump lips with his own, taste her the way he'd imagined doing for these past few weeks.

Then he took a closer look at her face. Her eyes were red, framed in dark shadow. It looked as if she might have been crying.

The thought that he might have caused those tears sent self-reproach shooting through him like lightning. For that alone, he supposed he would hear her out.

But it had to end there. His heart couldn't take much more.

Sierra half expected to have the door shut in her face when Dante opened it. For a horrifying moment, he looked as if he wanted to do just that. Right before he gave her a resigned sigh and crossed his arms over his bare chest.

Why did it have to be bare? Getting through what she planned was going to be difficult enough without the distraction of Dante's naked upper body in her line of sight. His hair still glistened wet. She must have rushed him from the shower. He hadn't toweled off completely, and moisture still clung to the muscled skin of his arms and torso. For a second she lost her train of thought. She also forgot the start of the speech she'd rehearsed all the way over here. Maybe she could ask him to go put a shirt on so that her brain could start functioning again.

"You called my mother to find out where I was?"

She could only nod.

"Why? What exactly are you doing here, Sierra?" he asked, not even bothering to invite her in. Sierra swallowed past her trepidation and forced herself to continue. She had to go through with this or she'd wonder for the rest of her life exactly what she'd thrown away so carelessly.

She held up the sketchbook she'd carried all the way up here from her apartment. "I wanted to get your opinion on something. If you have a minute."

Dante hesitated, his eyes skeptical as they glanced at the book in her hand then back to her face. He repeated the cycle twice more before he spoke. "I suppose I have a few minutes. Come in." He might have uttered the invitation, but Dante made no effort to move to let her inside.

Sierra stepped past him and into the room, brushing against his naked skin. Electricity shot through her core at the contact.

So not the time.

The man was not going to make things easy for her. Not that she could really blame him.

The room was dark, the blinds and curtains still drawn. His laptop screen lit up a small square in the corner. Paperwork was strewn about the floor. She knew Dante to be much tidier than the appearance of this room indicated. But what really alarmed her was the smattering of broken glass and mirror in front of the fireplace mantel.

"Did you have some kind of accident?"

"Something like that," Dante answered. "I tried to clean it up…" He trailed off. It was then that Sierra noticed the bandage on his hand.

He didn't give her a chance to ask about it. "Let's get this started then, shall we. I have a jet to catch."

Right. He was a busy man. And she was about to turn his life upside down. Hopefully.

"Sure thing." She walked over to the mahogany table in the center of the room and laid her sketchbook flat. A professional one this time, large with high quality drafting paper. Much different from the mini pocket-size ones she'd been sketching on back in Africa. This particular drawing deserved no less. She opened it up to the middle page.

Dante moved next to her to take a look. He stared at it blankly.

"What do you think?" she asked after several moments of silence.

Pinching the bridge of his nose, he released a long sigh. Sierra knew she was testing his patience. But this was the only way she could think of to say what she had to say without chickening out.

"I think it's a wedding dress," Dante finally answered after several more awkward beats. "For a bride."

She nodded. "That's right, it is."

"And?"

"Do you like it?"

He shrugged noncommittally. "It looks like a dress. With a long skirt. And a veil. Definitely a wedding dress."

She had to chuckle at that. "We've established that."

He turned away from the table to face her.

"Why are you showing it to me? I'm not exactly an expert on women's fashion. Let alone wedding dresses. Or any dresses for that matter."

She swallowed. This was so much harder than she'd even imagined it would be. "Well, the truth is, neither am I."

He gave a brisk shake of his head. "I'm sorry. I don't understand. You design clothes for a living."

"Yes, but wedding attire is an entirely different industry. I design for the runway, or for magazine shoots."

"Yet you drew this." He pointed to the open book.

"I did, yes."

He gave an exasperated shrug. "Do you want me to say I'm impressed. Yes, you're very talented. You didn't have to come all the way up here to hear me say that. I've said it several times over before now."

Sierra pulled out the nearest chair and sat down before her knees gave out.

"The thing is, I was hoping to wear something like this myself. But only if you like it. I think it might look pretty flattering. It's exactly the kind of dress I'd hope to wear on my wedding day."

His brow furrowed and he stared at her for so long that Sierra figured he really wasn't getting what she was trying to say. Then she watched as a glimmer of understanding flashed over his face.

His jaw dropped and he rubbed an open palm down his face.

"Sierra, just to be clear, are you saying what I think you're saying?"

She nodded, determined to take the chance she'd come here to take, no matter the consequences. "I'm saying that I love you. That I've loved you for as long as I can remember knowing you. And I wish I'd admitted it sooner." To herself and to him.

Dante squeezed his eyes shut, remained silent for so long that Sierra felt a trickle of apprehension run along her spine. Had she made a colossal mistake?

No. No mistake. Whatever Dante's reaction to her declaration, she'd had to get out in the open her true feelings for this man. It was beyond time.

Finally, when he opened his eyes to look at her again, she knew she'd had nothing to be apprehensive about. A wealth of emotion darkened their depths, his features awash with tenderness No man had ever looked at her that way. No one had. What a fool she'd been not to have seen it earlier—this man loved her! She should have seen it in his eyes, in the way he'd held her, in every word he'd spoken to her throughout the years. He proclaimed it out loud with his next words. "You have to know that I love you too. I always have, Sisi."

A torrent of affection flooded her system at his words. She'd only just sat down, but her jubilation had her jumping right back up again. "I guess women don't typically drop to one knee, but I will if you want." To his clear astonishment, she began to lower herself before Dante grabbed her by the wrist to lift her back up.

"Sierra, what are you doing?"

She grinned at him. "Isn't it obvious? I'm proposing."

Her breath caught in her throat at the expression that fell over his face at her words.

"Dante Angilera, please do me the honor of making me your wife. I'm going to need some help with the whole future queen thing, but I'm willing to do whatever it takes—"

Her words were interrupted when Dante cut her off by taking her upper arms and yanking her to him. Then his lips were on hers in a deep, crushing kiss. Sierra's arms flew around his neck, his damp skin wetting the front of her shirt. He cupped her behind, lifted her up onto the table in front of them and continued to kiss her some more.

When he finally let her go, Sierra didn't think she'd ever be able to catch her breath. It caught once more at the look on Dante's face. An ocean of emotion swam behind his eyes. "The wife part was all I needed to hear. And you would look amazing in any dress. Even a knee-length canvas tunic." Pulling her against him again, he delved into her mouth once more for a deep, mind-blowing kiss that melted her heart and her soul. When they finally parted, Sierra wasn't entirely sure she was back on earth and not on some heavenly plane where all her fantasies had just come true.

It took several long moments before she could speak again. "I take it that's a yes."

Dante didn't need any words when he answered her

EPILOGUE

GALEN ADDED ANOTHER layer of color to Sierra's lower lip, then pulled back. The smile she flashed in the mirror above her head was one of sheer joy. Sierra felt pretty joyful herself. She was living a true fairy tale. About to marry a crown prince. *Her* prince. More importantly, she was about to marry the man she'd always been in love with.

Next to them, Tracey clasped her hands against her chest, a lace veil draped over her forearm. The moment brought forth a wave of déjà vu. The last time Sierra was in this chair with these two women seemed a lifetime ago.

And now her new life was about to start.

She would do her best to not take a single moment of it for granted. Closing her eyes, she gave a silent nod to Rula. Her deceased friend had played a major role in the path that had led Sierra to this joyous moment. Not only through her journal of letters but also during her years of friendship.

"You look beautiful, Sierra," Galen said, giving her shoulder a squeeze and pulling her out of her contemplations.

"Absolutely lovely," Tracey agreed.

"I think it's obligatory to say that to the bride," Sierra said. "Plus a lot of it is your handiwork."

Galen waved her hand dismissively. "Nonsense. We're saying it because it's true. But I will take the compliment about my skills."

"As well you should," Sierra told her, gently standing up to avoid wrinkling the body of her bridal gown.

"Now, let's get this skirt and the veil on you," Tracey said, stepping forward with the items in question. "It's almost time."

Sierra didn't need the reminder; the butterflies in her stomach were doing that well enough. She was only slightly more nervous than the last time she'd been prepped by these ladies. She would never have guessed that morning of the news conference that the trip to Valhali would lead her here, about to finally tie herself to the only man she'd ever loved.

She couldn't wait to spend the rest of her life with him.

Tracey helped her slip the skirt and train of the gown on her then gently placed the tiara and veil combination atop her head. Galen made a few adjustments to her hair.

"You're ready," both women declared in unison.

Sierra took a fortifying breath then followed them to the door, around the porch to the back of the Melekhanna lodge where her father waited to walk her down the aisle. Her mother was in the front row of the audience chairs in front of the dais, probably on her third package of tissues. Both her parents had been beyond surprised at the announcement that she'd be marrying Dante. As was most of the world.

"The Ever Grieving Prince finally discovers new love!" read one headline.

The others were rather similar.

Little did anyone know their love wasn't new by any means. They'd just needed to find what was right there under their noses.

Sierra's father beamed at her when she made it to his side. He gave her a small peck on the cheek then led her down the steps, and onto the wooden pathway leading to the dais. Audible gasps sounded from the guests in attendance, which included a large number of fellow Nocerians, including Dante's mother and his father, who'd finally been given the medical clearance to resume travel, as well as so many dear friends she and Dante had made here in Valhali—Banti and his family, Nantu and Kaliha…even Tiejo had taken leave from his veterinary duties to be here. And no small amount of international press and photographers were hovering on the outer perimeter.

But Sierra hardly registered any of it. Her gaze was focused on the man standing waiting for her on the dais. Dante looked so handsome she thought she might forget to breathe. In his ceremonial royal dress, he looked every inch a regal leader who would be crowned king one day. More importantly, as far as Sierra was concerned, he would soon be her husband.

Dante couldn't believe his good fortune as he watched Sierra walking toward him. His soon to be wife. He'd be hard-pressed to find the words to describe her. A vision. It was the only description that came to mind. So much time wasted. He should have admitted years ago that she was always the only woman for him.

But the only thing he wanted to focus on right now was the joy of this day. Even nature seemed to be helping them to celebrate. The setting sun cast a burst of color in the sky above them. The hum of the cicadas seemed to rise and fall in tempo, almost as if performing a tune in their honor. Or maybe he was simply being fanciful because he was simply so happy.

There was no other location better for their wedding day. Valhali was where they'd both found the courage to finally acknowledge their true feelings and stop resisting the mutual pull of their love.

As a bonus, the publicity would serve as a further boost for NEWEF. Maman was very pleased about that. Not to mention the romantic setting with such stunning views as a backdrop.

Once they'd said their vows and bowed to the applause from the audience, Dante led her to the head table to await the festivities.

The dancers from their first night here appeared and began a ceremonial matrimony dance in their honor. Dante took advantage of the diverted attention to focus on his beautiful bride. Splaying his hand on her lower back, he turned her toward him and pulled her closer. Her response was immediate. She lifted her chin and met his lips for a soul-shattering kiss that had his insides turning to lava. When he finally managed to begrudgingly pull away, he didn't think he could bear the loss.

Sierra gave him a knowing look, the desire in her eyes matching his own.

Pretty soon, several of their guests had joined the dancers on the floor. Just as he and Sierra had on that night many months ago.

"I'm so grateful that so many friends and loved ones are able to be here to celebrate with us," Sierra said.

Dante nodded. "Me too. Father seems to be

back to his old energetic ways. One of his doctors speculated that our wedding gave him a positive boost toward recovery."

"Thank heavens."

"Though I think there might be at least one uninvited guest," Dante declared with mock seriousness.

Sierra pulled back with an alarmed expression. "Oh? Who?"

He pointed to the tree line in the distance. "I'm pretty sure my friend the vervet monkey is in that tree just waiting to make his move and steal a banana from the buffet."

Sierra chuckled and snuggled in tighter against his shoulder.

"Would you like to dance?" he asked his bride after a few moments of simply enjoying her closeness and warmth. "The way we did all those months ago?"

"In a few moments," she answered. "Right now I just want to sit here next to you."

That was fine with him. "As you wish, Princess Sisi," he told her, playfully tapping her nose.

Dante draped his arm around her shoulders and they watched the dancers.

"When we do dance, please remind me to take the skirt and train off," Sierra said, settling tighter against him. Dante had to resist the urge to pull her onto his lap and kiss her until neither one of them could breathe. Patience. He would have to wait until they were alone together that night unfortunately. Sierra was worth the wait.

"We don't need a replay of my clumsiness that night," she added.

He chuckled at that. "I wouldn't complain. I rather enjoy catching the woman I love in my arms."

He would be prepared to catch her for the rest of their lives together.

* * * * *

If you enjoyed this story,
check out these other great reads
from Nina Singh

Two Weeks to Tempt the Tycoon
Caribbean Contract with Her Boss
Wearing His Ring till Christmas
Whisked into the Billionaire's World

All available now!